I'M A NOTICER.
I NOTICE THINGS.

FOR INSTANCE, I
NOTICED YOU OPENED
THIS BOOK.

Marty Pants

KEEP YOUR PAWS OFF!

Mark Parisi

HARPER

An Imprint of HarperCollinsPublishers

To Jen–
The best thing I ever had a hand in creating.

Marty Pants #2: Keep Your Paws Off!
Copyright © 2017 by Mark Parisi
All rights reserved. Printed in the United States of America.
No part of this book may be used or reproduced in any manner whatsoever without written permission except in the case of brief quotations embodied in critical articles and reviews. For information address HarperCollins Children's Books, a division of HarperCollins Publishers, 195 Broadway, New York, NY 10007.
www.harpercollinschildrens.com
Library of Congress Control Number: 2017934808
ISBN 978-0-06-242778-6
Typography by Joe Merkel
18 19 20 21 22 CG/LSCH 10 9 8 7 6 5 4 3 2 1
❖
First Edition

CHAPTER 0

getting ahead of myself

My life's going downhill. Literally!

It's the night of the full moon, and things are spinning out of control!

The people who laughed at me are now screaming and running. What they are witnessing will be talked about for generations!

How did I get in this hairy situation? Let me tell you how it started.

every picture tells a story

I need to find a baby photo for the class yearbook. Even though I was a totally adorable baby, there don't seem to be many pictures of me.

My sister, Erica, was born first. Here are her baby pictures.

Here are mine.

I guess that's how it goes when you're the second child. But once I'm a famous artist, my baby pictures will be like *gold*, and my parents will regret not having more.

Flipping through the box, I come across an old photo of me with my sister. Look how well we used to get along.

These days it's a little different.
As if to make my point, Erica bursts into my room.

MARTY!

MY KIND, LOVING SISTER

She knows how to make an entrance.

"GET YOUR PSYCHO CAT OUT OF MY BACK-PACK!"

"He's just playing," I tell her.

"MAAAARTYYY!"

"Fine," I say. "Come here, Jerome!"

Jerome leaps over to me, and I give him a stern talking-to.

GOOD BOY

"Control your beast!" Erica snaps as she marches off to annoy someone else.

For some unexplained reason, Jerome really likes Erica's backpack.*

Jerome's my cat and best bud. He was given to me by a neighbor years ago.

For free. No strings attached.

I'm still not sure why she decided to be so generous.

* It might be because I hid catnip in an inside pocket, but that's just a guess.

NEIGHBOR

I notice poor Jerome has some paper stuck in his claws.* He was digging through Erica's backpack, so it must be from one of her school papers.

Like her A+ homework assignments. Or her A+ tests. Or her A+ projects. Or her A+ . . .

Wait.

I take a closer look and realize it isn't from her schoolwork.

It's from her DIARY!

RANDOM PHOTOS

* Like I said, I'm a noticer. I notice things.

I've only seen Erica's diary from a distance, but I recognize the gold-trimmed page.

And diaries are only for one thing.

Should I read it? No.

Will I read it?

Of course I will.

I place the ripped diary fragment under my lamp to soak in some sinister sister secrets.

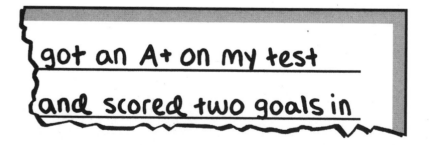

got an A+ on my test
and scored two goals in

Those aren't secrets! That's just bragging! Erica doesn't even know how to do a diary properly!

I'm ready to toss it out but notice there's also something written on the other side.

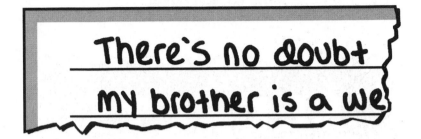

i am what we is

Huh? Erica's writing secrets about me?! Without my permission?

We . . .

What could that mean?

What does she know about me? What am I that starts with we . . . ?

My mind runs through the possibilities.

WEIGHT LIFTER

WELDER

WEATHERMAN

WEDDING SINGER

WEEPING WILLOW

WEEDWACKER

I'm fairly confident I'm none of those. This leaves me with only one option. Read the rest of Erica's diary!

How? Jerome got me part of it, right? He can get me the rest!

"Jerome! Fetch Erica's diary!"

Jerome scampers out of the room, and he's back in a flash. But he doesn't quite get what I'm after.

He keeps trying.

After several more tries, I can tell my dad is starting to get annoyed.

I guess I need to steal her diary myself.
I'll be patient and choose the exact perfect moment.
That moment is *now*.

CHAPTER 3
step by step, inch by inch

I sneak into Erica's room dressed as a ninja. I see her clearly. She's reading a book about werewolves, but she can't see me because, like I said, I'm dressed as a ninja.

I inch closer to her backpack and . . .

My sister has keener senses than I anticipated. It appears she's exceptionally skilled at noticing things, just like I am.

I slowly retreat backward out of the room. "And shut the door!" she snaps.

This is going to be harder than I thought.

CHAPTER 4

drawing conclusions

Getting my hands on Erica's diary will be a challenge, but I can't give up.

Did Pablo Picasso give up when he failed anatomy?

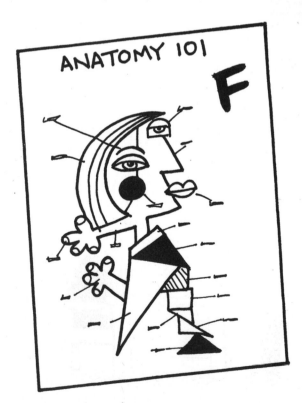

Did Sandro Botticelli give up when he failed biology?

Did Walt Disney give up when he failed zoology?

No. They kept going against all odds. And that's what
I need to do.

But how can I devise a devious diary-stealing strategy
slick enough to trick my sister?*

I could hire a professional thief to do the job for me,
but that has a potential downside.

* Try saying that ten times fast.

This will take some thought, so I sink into my thinking place, the beanbag of solitude, and try to concentrate.

But it's hard to do your serious thinking when someone is next to you making noises and having fun.

Jerome bats one photo directly into my lap. I pick it up. It's an old picture of my parents and me at the beach when I was a toddler.

Look how cute I am.

My adorability shines through anything.

I pick up another, and it's of me playing in the sand. I look even cuter, if that's possible.

Hold everything!
I'm having an *epidemic*!

No, that's the wrong word.

I run to the top of the stairs.

"DAD!" I yell down. "What do you have when your brain suddenly realizes something important? It starts with an *e*!"

"A eureka moment?" my dad guesses.

"That's not the one I mean."

"An epiphany?"

"Yes! Thanks, Dad!"

I get back in my beanbag. I'm having an *epiphany*!

Erica was on her bed reading a book. And what was the book about? Werewolves.

And what are the first two letters of *werewolf*?

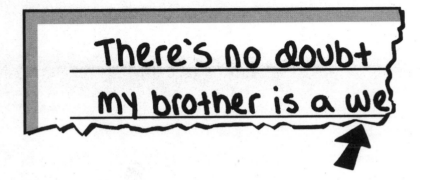

CHAPTER 5

talk talk

Is it possible I could be a werewolf and not even know it? I need to talk this through with someone smart.

I ride my bike to Parker's house.

Yes, that's a frog. Bikes are hard to draw, so I draw frogs instead.

I know what you're thinking. How can I be a brilliant artist and still have trouble with bikes?

Let me put it this way.

Here's a famous painting by an artist named René Magritte.

He obviously had trouble with faces, yet he's still considered a brilliant artist. Enough said.

I get to Parker's and leave my bike on the side of the garage.

I always consult Parker when stuff gets real. She wants to be a psychologist and practices her craft on me. It works out well for both of us.*

I knock on the door, but there's no answer.

I'm ready to leave when I hear, "Hey, Marty!"

It's Parker's voice, but I don't see her anywhere. Has she mastered invisibility? Is she now part of the spirit realm?

* But it really works better for her because I'm such an interesting patient.

Or is she on the roof of the garage? That was my next guess.

"Hey, Parker," I say. "Got a minute?"

"Anytime," she says. "Is this personal or professional?"

"Professional," I answer, and hold this in the air.

"Excellent," Parker says. "Meet you inside!"

I let myself in. Her dad doesn't seem to be home.

I usually lie down on the couch for these sessions, but today it's covered in piles of laundry.

I find the next suitable location.

Parker climbs in the window and pulls up a chair. "Glad to see you made yourself comfortable, Marty."

"It's not that comfortable."

"Well?" she says. "What's today's topic? The anticipation is killing me."

"It's a doozy," I tell her.

"It always is, Mr. Marty."

How can I break this to her? "Parker," I say. "I think I'm a werewolf."

"Did I just hear you right?"

"Did you just hear me say 'I think I'm a werewolf'?"

"Yes."

"Then your hearing is fine."

"Good. I was worried."

"Yes, hearing is important," I explain.

"It sure is, especially if there's a werewolf on the loose."

"I know. Like me."

"So, pardon me for asking," Parker says.

"Consider yourself pardoned," I tell her.

"Should I be concerned that you're about to rip me to shreds?"

"Not until the next full moon, I suppose."

"That's a relief," she says. "So, what makes you think you're a werewolf?"

"It makes sense."

"You being a werewolf makes sense?"

"Once you look at all the evidence," I explain, and present her with Exhibit A. "This is from my sister's diary."

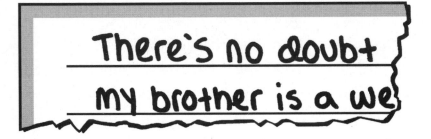

There's no doubt
my brother is a we

I give her a couple of seconds to examine it, then say, "In case you don't know, *w* and *e* are the first two letters of werewolf."

"Can't argue with that," Parker agrees. "But don't you have to be bitten by a werewolf to become one?"

"Not if it runs in the family," I explain. "And I have reason to believe it does."

I present her with Exhibit B.

"You're adorable!" Parker notes correctly.

"Very perceptive," I say. "But tear your eyes away from my cuteness, and look at the guy behind me."

"Who's that?"

"It has to be my uncle Harry S. Wolfman or someone like that. Just look at him! I figure I got the werewolf gene from him."

"You have wild theories," Parker says.

"It's science."

"So, you think your whole family are werewolves?"

"My instincts say it's just me," I tell her. "And Parker, please keep this on the down low. I don't want to cause a nationwide panic."

"Naturally," Parker promises. "But I have another question."

"You mean, how could someone so adorable be a werewolf?"

"Sure. That. And also, why haven't you ever actually, you know, transformed into a werewolf?"

RAAH!

LIKE THIS

"I thought about that," I say. "I just had a birthday. I must finally be old enough for the werewolf gene to kick in!"

"Got it. And your sister knows you're a werewolf, how, exactly?"

"There are a lot of unanswered questions," I admit. "I'm going to get the answers tonight, when I read Erica's diary."

"Wow! That should make things exciting at your house!"

"I'll let you know."

"Why don't you just ask Erica what she wrote?"

"Parker, Parker, Parker," I say, rolling my head side to side. "You should know you can't just ask a girl what she wrote in her diary. I mean, will you tell me what you wrote in *your* diary?"

"GET OUT!" Parker shouts.

"See?" I say.

"I MEAN, LITERALLY! GET OUT! MY DAD JUST GOT HOME!"

CHAPTER 6

speaking in tongues

There's something important to know about Parker's dad.

IF ANY BOYS ARE HERE WHEN I'M NOT HOME...

I'LL USE THEIR SKIN AND BONES TO MAKE FURNITURE!

I still don't know if he was serious, but it's certainly not worth the risk.

I zip out the side door!

And it's pitch-black outside!

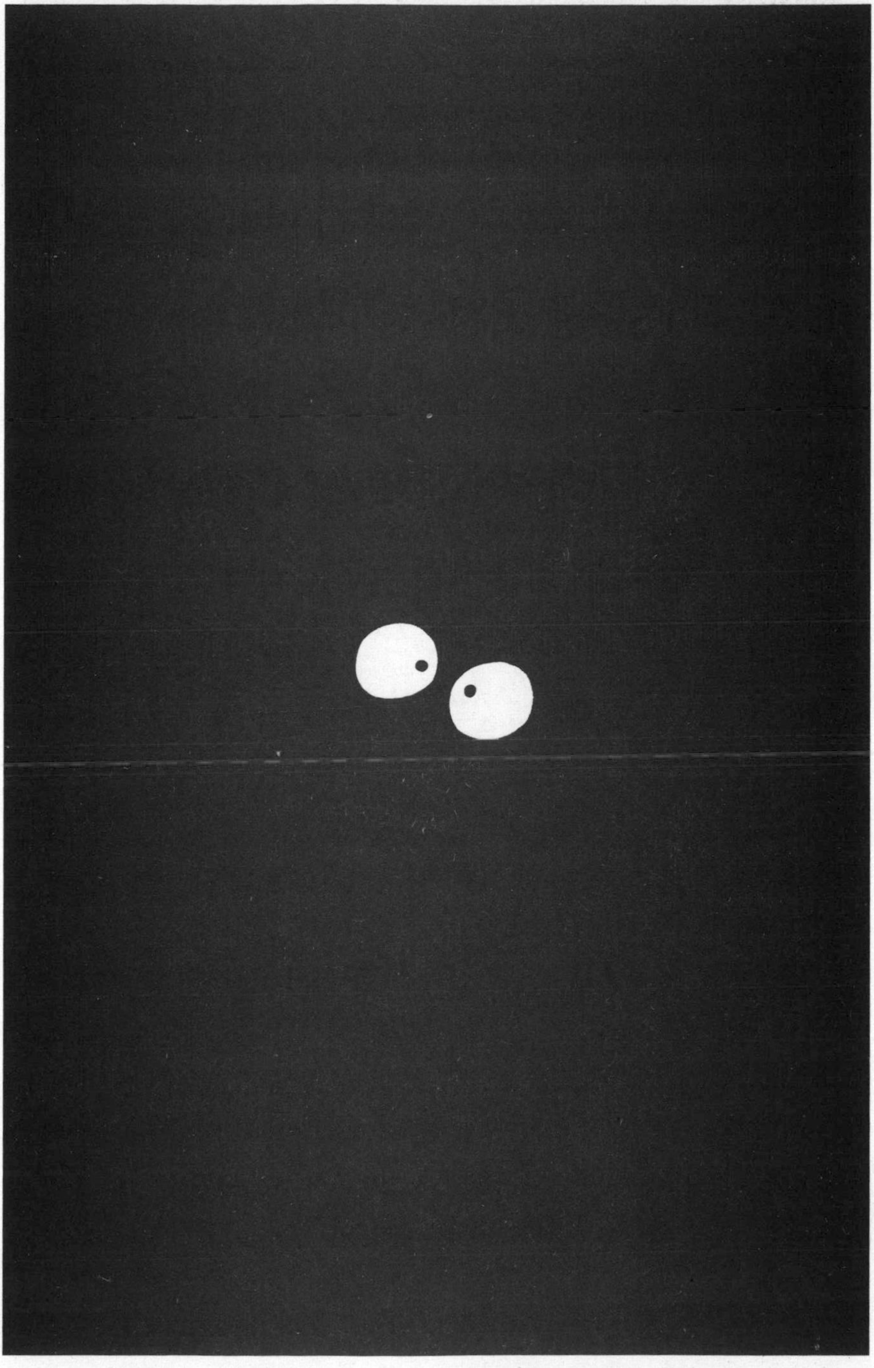

How long was I at Parker's??

I slowly realize I'm not outside at all. I'm in the garage.

I fumble around and knock something over. Oops.

I need to be careful not to make too much noise and draw attention to myself.

Or I might end up like this.

I put my hands out and finally find a stool to sit on. I hope it's nobody I know.

I'm getting creeped out sitting here alone in the dark but decide to wait for Parker to tell me when the coast is clear.

Gurk! What was that? I heard something next to me!

Just as I'm about to freak out, I feel something on my lips.

A kiss!

No way!

Parker tricked me into the dark garage so she could kiss me?

I didn't know she liked me that way.

It would be rude not to kiss back, right? And I don't want to be rude.

Suddenly, the light comes on.

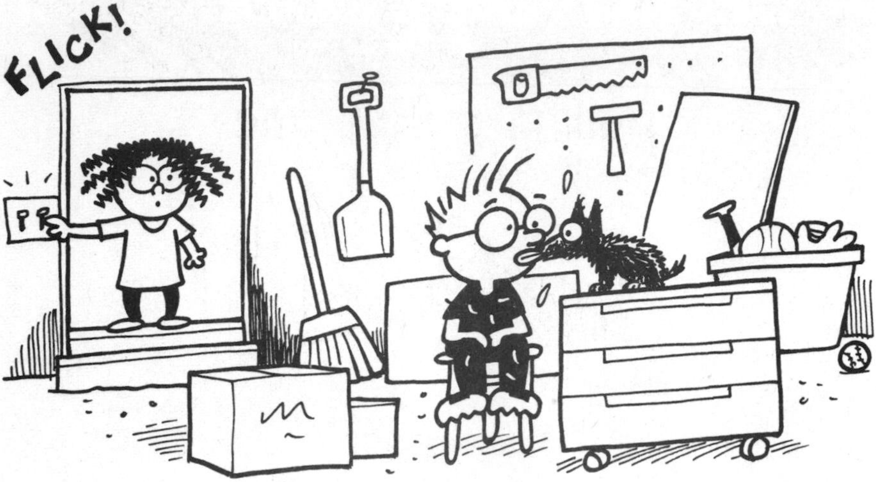
FLICK!

CHAPTER 1
pulling a fast one

"Awwwww, sweet!" Parker says.

I instantly become very aware of the taste of dog saliva in my mouth.

"He's a stray," Parker tells me. "I named him Dewey and leave out food sometimes. Isn't he cute?"

"Adorable! That's why I was kissing him!" I say, regretting it instantly.

"I'm impressed. He's so shy that I haven't even been able to pet him."

"Where'd he go?" I ask, looking around.

"Through that loose board. I need to convince my dad to let me keep him."

"Speaking of your dad . . ."

"Right! You better go, Marty. He could come in here at any moment. And he's been talking about wanting a new armoire."

I don't know what an armoire is, and this isn't the way I want to find out!

I squeeze out through the loose board, spitting on the ground the whole time.

I spit again. And again and again and again.*

Then I hear a familiar voice.

* Et cetera.

Gurk! It's Salvador Ack! Or as I call him in my head, Peach Fuzz. It's because of his stupid peach-fuzz mustache. Meanwhile, he refers to me as Wetty Pants. He's a high school kid who likes to teach me lessons.

I've learned a lot from him over the years:

What a wet willie is . . .

What a wedgie is . . .

What it looks
like on the inside
of a toilet . . .

And now Peach Fuzz thinks I'm making fun of him!
Why? Because I'm spitting.

Spitting is kind of his thing. It's practically his trade-mark.

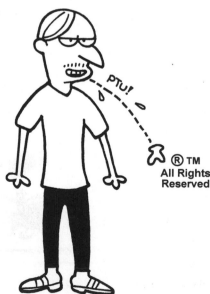

I'll just explain myself.

"I'm not making fun of you, Salvador! I'm spitting because I just made out with a puppy dog!"

I see no way this explanation is going to help me. Peach Fuzz spits on the ground and walks over to my bike. He lets the air out of one of my tires.

"I thinks ya need ta be tawt a lessun, Weddy Pants," Peach Fuzz says as he balls up his fists.

It so happens I'm not really in the mood for learning. I'm in the mood for running! I take off, and Peach Fuzz chases me.

But without my bike, I'm a sitting duck! I know he'll catch me on foot. He always does.

But somehow I get away this time!

When I get home, I'm completely out of breath and collapse into my beanbag of solitude.

How did I manage to escape Peach Fuzz without my bike?

I think about it and suddenly have an epiphany.

CHAPTER 8

listomania

My werewolf powers must be kicking in!

The responsible thing to do is make a list of characteristics that relate to werewolfism and see how many of the telltale signs I'm already showing.

I come up with the 12 Werewolf Symptoms.

THE 12 WEREWOLF SYMPTOMS

○ 1. SUPERHUMAN SPEED

2. ATTRACTION TO CANINES

3. FANGS

4. HOWLING

5. RIPPED CLOTHES

○ 6. AGGRESSION

7. HAIRINESS

8. FLEAS

9. GROWLING

10. CRAVING FOR MEAT

○ 11. DROOLING

12. SUPERHUMAN STRENGTH

I totally outran Peach Fuzz, and I totally made out with that dog, so I can check off the first two items right away.

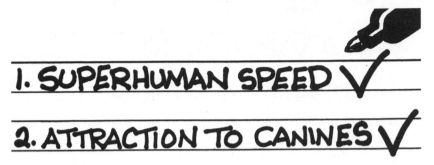

1. SUPERHUMAN SPEED ✓

2. ATTRACTION TO CANINES ✓

But this is a long list. I still might be okay.

If this *entire* list gets crossed off, then it becomes official. I'm on a one-way trip to werewolfville.

In the meantime, I need to keep an open mind. And there's one other thing that needs to be opened.

Something I've only seen from a distance.

ERICA'S DIARY

smarty pants

Erica is spouting random facts at the dinner table because she's going to participate in a History Trivia Contest in another city. She just needs to raise money for the entry fee.

The winner gets a college scholarship. Or a beach towel—I can't remember.

Amazing how my sister can sit calmly next to me, all the while knowing I'm a werewolf.

I suppose there's a minuscule chance that I'm not really a werewolf, and there's another explanation for everything.

I need to check when the next full moon is. That's kind of important!

And my bike is still at Parker's. What will her dad do if he finds a boy's bike on the side of his house?

My first priority should be to read Erica's diary. That's what I need to focus on.

"Marty? Marty?"

Gurk! Apparently, my mom's been talking to me and expects an answer.

Now it's my turn to impress everyone with my knowledge.

BABOONS HAVE BRIGHT RED BUTTS!

CHAPTER 10

bite off more than you can chew

I need to know what Erica wrote about me. I spend my Sunday developing a plan to make Erica leave the house so I can steal* her diary.

There are four simple steps to my plan.

* Maybe "borrow without permission" is a better term.

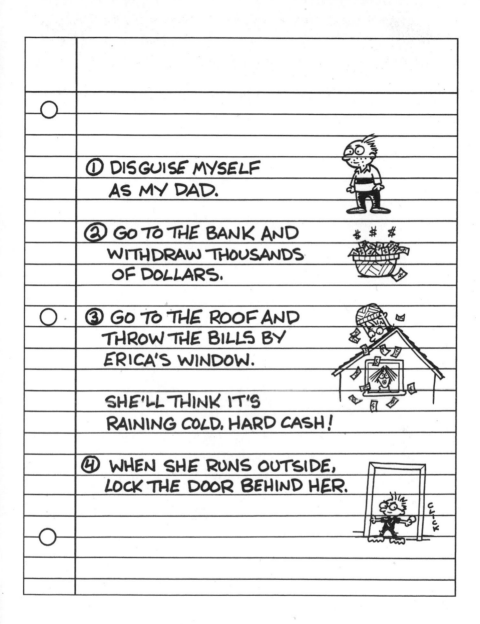

① DISGUISE MYSELF AS MY DAD.

② GO TO THE BANK AND WITHDRAW THOUSANDS OF DOLLARS.

③ GO TO THE ROOF AND THROW THE BILLS BY ERICA'S WINDOW.

SHE'LL THINK IT'S RAINING COLD, HARD CASH!

④ WHEN SHE RUNS OUTSIDE, LOCK THE DOOR BEHIND HER.

Then I'll run to her room!
It's the perfect plan to get Erica outside the house!

That works, too.

Once I'm sure Erica is gone, I tiptoe down the hall to her door.

As you can see, she's always changing the spelling of her name. No one knows why.

I quietly turn the knob and peek inside.

It's inconceivable how neat she keeps her room. So, of course, I notice her backpack right away.

If she kept her room like mine, it would have been much harder to spot.

There's a lesson in there somewhere.

I enter her room and quietly put one foot in front of the other.

Soon, I'm standing directly over her backpack. Is her diary still inside?

I take a deep breath and unzip the main compartment slowly and dramatically.

And there it is!

Erica's book of secrets!

I have it in my hands!

I can finally read everything she wrote about me. Except . . . Gurk! It's locked!

Pretty sneaky, sis.

But all she's done is make me want to read it even more.

I glance around the room, wondering where Erica would hide an important key.

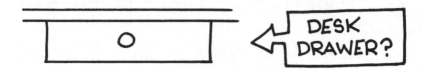

That's too obvious.

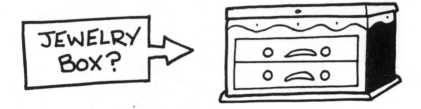

That's the last place you'd put something valuable.

Honestly, I'm afraid of what's in there.

I decided to start my search here.

I check underneath the first candy bar.

I don't see a key. But it could be under that next candy bar.

Not there, either.

But I need to be thorough. It could be under *any* of these candy bars.

Through the process of elimination, I determine the key is not in the box.

Next stop: Erica's desk drawer.

MARTY, WHAT ARE YOU DOING IN THERE?

truthiness

My brain freezes for a moment. Should I just tell my dad the truth?

Should I say I'm here to steal Erica's diary? To find out if I'm a werewolf?

In first grade, my teacher had a theory.

HONESTY IS THE BEST POLICY!

She even had us do an assignment on the subject. This was mine:

HONESTY IS THE BEST POLICY

STARRING

PINOCCHIO AND MARTY

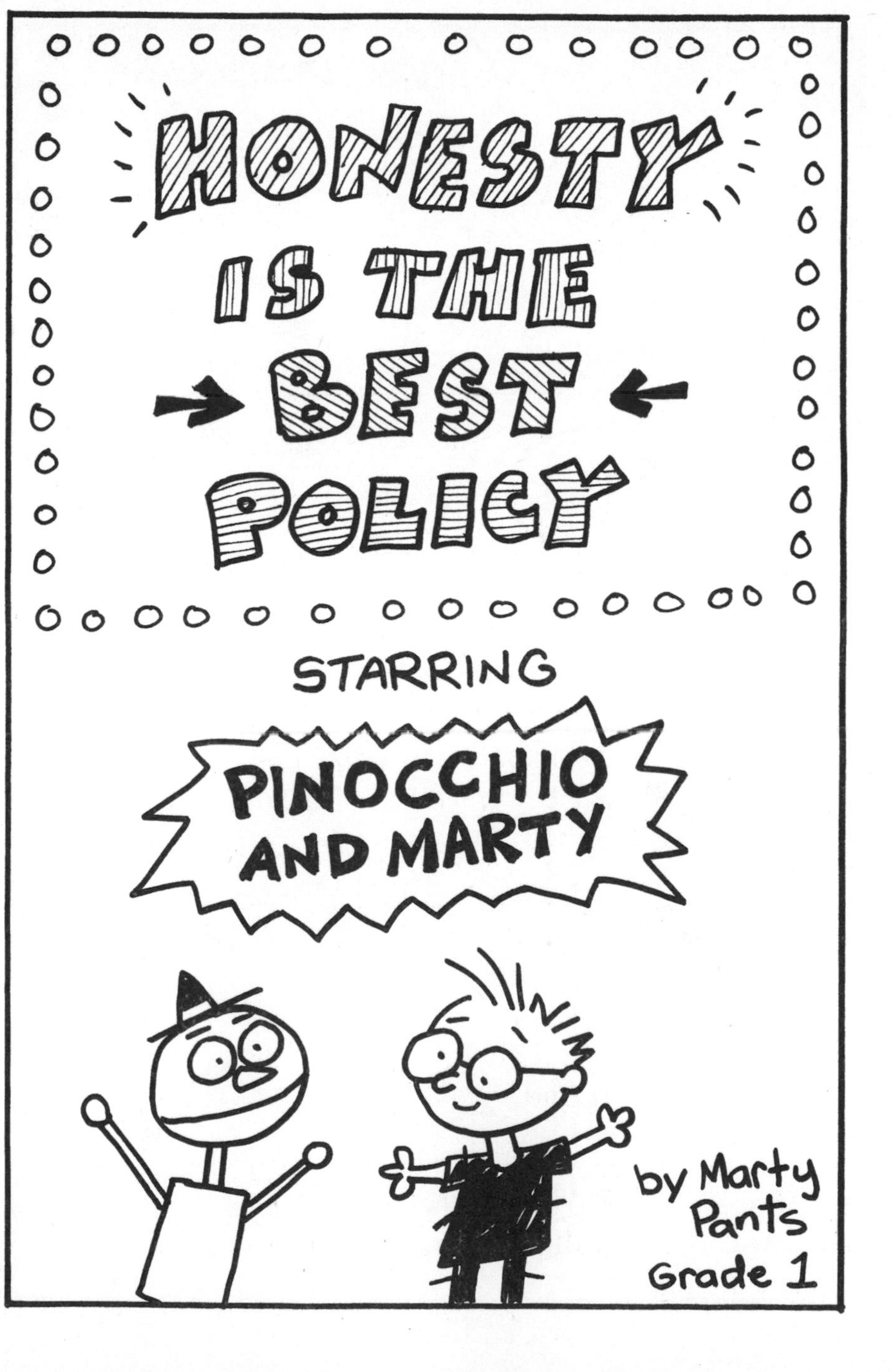

by Marty Pants
Grade 1

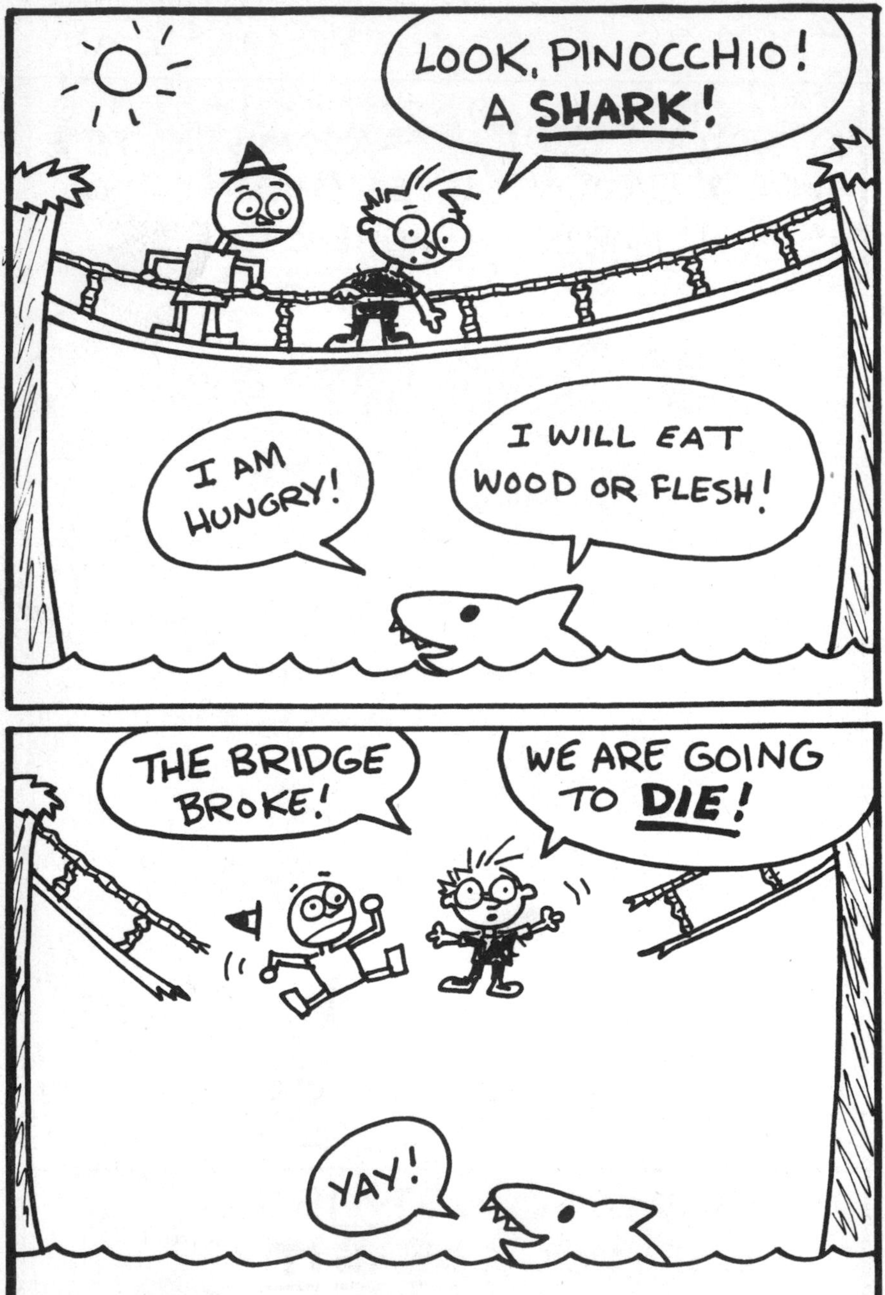
LOOK, PINOCCHIO! A **SHARK**!
I AM HUNGRY!
I WILL EAT WOOD OR FLESH!
THE BRIDGE BROKE!
WE ARE GOING TO **DIE**!
YAY!

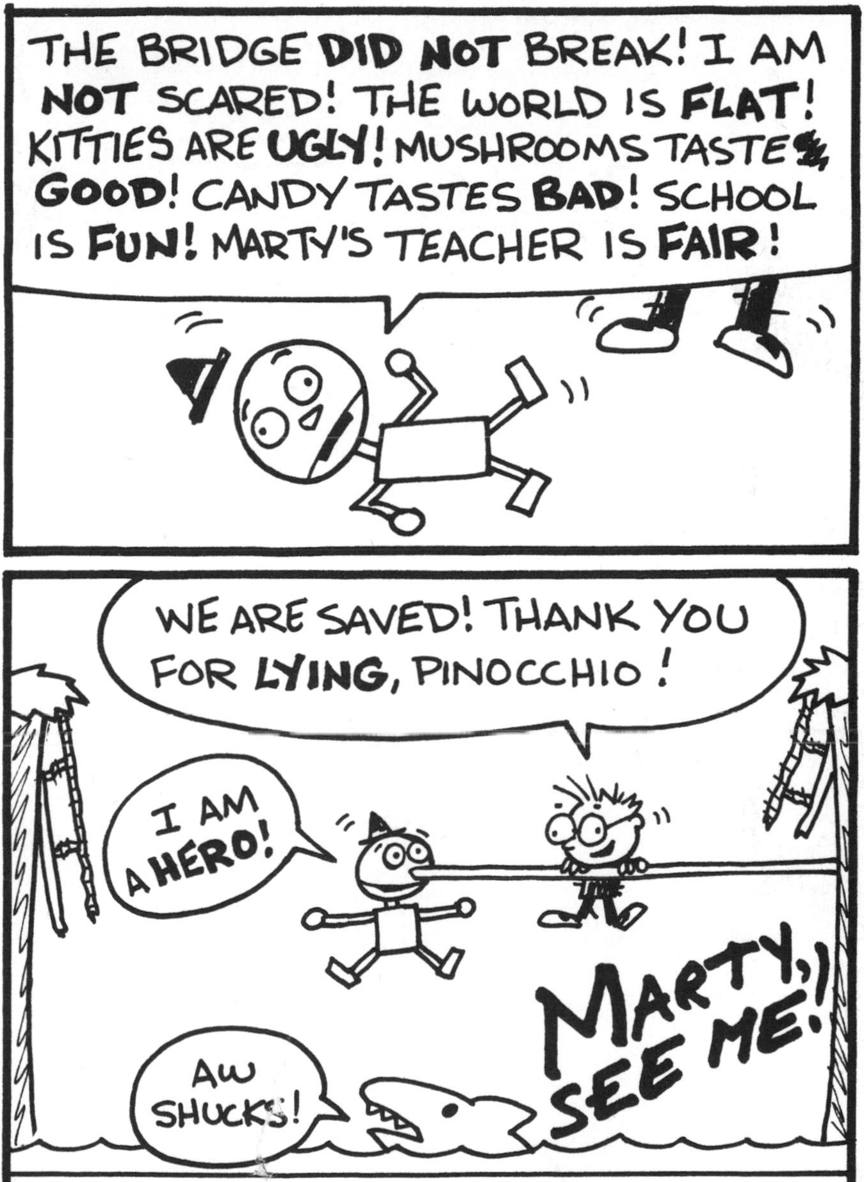
THE BRIDGE DID NOT BREAK! I AM NOT SCARED! THE WORLD IS FLAT! KITTIES ARE UGLY! MUSHROOMS TASTE GOOD! CANDY TASTES BAD! SCHOOL IS FUN! MARTY'S TEACHER IS FAIR!
WE ARE SAVED! THANK YOU FOR LYING, PINOCCHIO!
I AM A HERO!
MARTY, SEE ME!
AW SHUCKS!
MORAL: HONESTY IS THE BEST POLICY. OR IS IT???

I didn't do very well on that assignment.

I turn to face my dad and casually drop Erica's diary into the nearest hiding place.

I cover it with the empty wrappers.

"Just cleaning up," I say.

"You ate all of Erica's candy?!"

"I'll pay for it, Dad. Now, tell me about the awesome music they had when you were a kid!"

This is the easiest way to get my dad off any subject.

My dad instantly launches into long, detailed descriptions of the concerts he went to, the albums he bought, the bands he . . .

Next thing I know, I wake up in my bed. And my dad's still talking!

I'm too groggy to sit up. "Dad, I surrender."

"I paid Erica for all those candy bars, Marty, but it's coming out of your allowance."

"Firm, but fair," I say.

"Good night, Marty," my dad says. "And stay out of Erica's room."

Gurk! The diary is still in the box!

"Dad?" I say sweetly. "Can I have the empty candy box? For Jerome?"

"That's up to Erica. Good night, Marty."

over a barrel

Next morning, I wake up earlier than usual. This may be the first time I've ever beaten Erica to the bathroom.

I'm about to brush my teeth and notice that four of them look awfully pointy.

Erica bangs on the door. "DAD! MARTY'S HOGGING THE BATHROOM!"

"Stop hogging the bathroom, Marty," my dad says automatically.

I open the door a crack and point to my mouth. "Erica, do these teeth look pointier than the others?"

Maybe I can trick Erica into spilling some pertinent information.

"Duh. Those are your canine teeth, weirdo," she says. Then she grabs my arm and yanks me out of the bathroom.

Canine teeth?

So *that's* how she figured out I'm becoming a werewolf. She noticed I have the teeth of a canine!

Her advanced ability to notice things might rival my own.

Time to check another item off my list of The 12 Werewolf Symptoms.

3. FANGS ✓

As soon as I hear the shower go on, I scoot over to Erica's room. Time to fish her diary out of the candy box.

But there's one problem.

NO BOX!

I sprint downstairs. "Dad! Candy box! Where?"

"Erica threw it away, Marty."

"But I WANTED that!"

I hear loud noises coming from the street and peer out the window.

Our trash barrel is lying on the sidewalk. Empty.

And a garbage truck is driving off!

I can see the candy box half buried in the back of the truck!

"NOOOOOO! THE BOX! THE BOX!!" I scream.

My dad looks up from his cereal.

"Aren't you overreacting a bit? We'll get you a different box."

"But... that particular box... it should be RECYCLED!" I answer back. "I MUST SAVE THE PLANET!"

I zip over to the front door.

I'm so frazzled, I push instead of pull. I turn the bolt and lock the door instead of unlocking it.

When I finally remember how a door works, I dash outside.

But the garbage truck is finished with our neighborhood, and it's already out of sight!

I bet I can catch it with my superhuman werewolf speed!

I've fallen down many times in my life. Too many to count. But I don't think I've ever made that sound before. I limp back into the house and update my list.

4. HOWLING ✓

CHAPTER 13

listlessness

Time to face facts. The diary is gone! And Erica won't stop reminding me.

So rude of her. She has no consideration for how important it was to me!

At least I still have my list. And the evidence is mounting.

THE 12 WEREWOLF SYMPTOMS

- 1. SUPERHUMAN SPEED ✓
- 2. ATTRACTION TO CANINES ✓
- 3. FANGS ✓
- 4. HOWLING ✓
- 5. RIPPED CLOTHES
- 6. AGGRESSION
- 7. HAIRINESS
- 8. FLEAS
- 9. GROWLING
- 10. CRAVING FOR MEAT
- 11. DROOLING
- 12. SUPERHUMAN STRENGTH

I meet Roongrat on the way to school and wonder if he notices anything different about me.

I sure notice something different about him.

"Why are you dressed in a tux?" I ask.

"It's picture day, Marty."

"That's today?"

"It's the most important day of our school experience," Roongrat goes on. "The better dressed you are, the more cash you'll make as a adult."

Here he goes. Typical Roongrat.

"Bosses make monetary salary decisions based on the neatness quotient of your school photographs," he adds. "It's an established fact."

Roongrat is my know-it-all friend who just makes stuff up. But he says things so confidently, I think he really believes everything he says.

"I'll obviously receive a plethora of job offers," he tells me. "As for you, Marty . . ."

"I don't need to dress well," I say proudly. "I'm going to be a professional artist."

"Not one that makes money," he says.

As usual, Roongrat doesn't know what he's talking about. I'll be one of the all-time greats, so my art will bring in gobs of money.

Van Gogh's paintings sell for millions.

Wait! I'm having another epiphany!

I might be able to figure out if I'm a werewolf right here and now.

Roongrat is so full of baloney that I basically believe the *opposite* of whatever he says.

Therefore, if he says werewolves are real, that's practically a *guarantee* that werewolves are *not* real!

"Roongrat," I say. "What do you have to say on the subject of werewolves?"

How he answers this question could be crucial to my future.

"Well," Roongrat starts. "There was a food industry scandal a few years back. Scientists found chunks of werewolf DNA in hamburger meat. Unicorn DNA, too. It was all kept hush-hush, so you've probably never heard about it."

"Right, right," I say slowly. "So, just to be clear, Roongrat, in your mind werewolves totally exist and are totally real?"

"Totally," he says confidently. "It's a fact."

Sweet!

If Roongrat thinks werewolves are real, then ipso facto werewolves are *not* real!

This logic has never failed me before.

So, that settles it. As of right now, I don't believe in werewolves.*

Guess I won't be needing this list anymore.

* Or unicorns.

CHAPTER 14

being human

Before class starts, I dig something out of my backpack and hand it to Parker.

COUPON 2
GOOD FOR ONE
SESSION WITH

Parker Fedora, PhD
(Personal Head Doctor)

"Got a minute?" I ask.

"Sure thing, Marty! What's up now?"

I get into position.

"Believe it or not," I whisper so the other students can't overhear, "I'm not a werewolf."

"Good to know! Did you actually read your sister's diary?"

"No. It's probably being eaten by worms as we speak."

"Worms?"

"It accidentally got tossed in the garbage," I tell her. "And, surprisingly, chasing garbage trucks isn't as fun as it sounds. I fell."

"Ah, so that explains it," Parker says.

"Explains what?"

She's right.

And then I notice I'm the only one in class who's not dressed up.

And Parker looks especially nice today. I should say something.

Gurk! Simon stole my line!

"Thanks, Simon!" Parker says.

Yeah, thanks a lot, Simon! Now I need to think of a completely different compliment to give Parker.

I don't think she heard my sweet talk, though, because Simon won't shut up. He's interrupting my session time!

Simon's not exactly my favorite person. In fact, I loathe Simon.

Why do I say *loathe*? Because my mom doesn't like it when I say *hate*.

To me, loathe means the same thing, but for some reason my mom's okay with it.

Simon's trying to show off by drawing on Parker's notebook.

Without even looking, I know exactly what he's drawing. It's a well-known cartoon character.

That's right. AnemoneBob TrapezoidShorts.* How do I know?

Am I a mind reader? No.

It's because that's all Simon *ever* draws!

---

* For legal reasons, this is what I'll call him. You know the character I mean. I know you do.

Need proof? Here are the doodles in his notebook.

This is the jersey he designed for our soccer team.

And this is his caricature of our teacher, Mr. McPhee.

That looks nothing like McPhee! *This* is what McPhee looks like.

CHAPTER 15

all you need is loathe

Simon is a one-trick pony. Yet, for reasons I'll never understand, he's considered the school artist.

That title should rightfully be mine! And it almost was.

I got a big break and was supposed to paint a mural in the front hall of the school.

Of course, Simon loathed the idea, so he came by to discuss my health.

"Are you feeling okay, Marty?" he asked.

"Yeah, why?"

He didn't stop there.

"You'll always be an amateur, Marty."

"You don't have what it takes to be a pro, Marty."

"No one will ever pay you for your crap, Marty."

"That looks like something I stepped in, Marty."

When I'd finally had enough of Simon the Stupid Art Critic, I snapped and let him have it.

"GO WASH A MONKEY!" I yelled.

I still have no idea what that means, but it captured how I felt.

"Ha-ha! That makes no sense!" Simon sneered. "Just like your art!"

He laughed and walked away. But he wasn't done.

"You know your problem, Marty?" he said from down the hall. "You don't understand art!"

That had to be the dumbest thing I'd ever heard. If there's one thing I understand, it's *art*!

Art is about expressing yourself. So I decided to express myself.

Unfortunately, not everyone understands art as well as I do.

McPhee was not amused by my artistic expression, and I lost my mural privileges.

Because of *Simon*. That monkey washer.

Even now, as I sit here at my desk, it's like I can still hear McPhee shouting my name.

"MARTY!"

It sounds so clear.

"MARTY! Stop daydreaming!"

CHAPTER 16

picture yourself

"Snap out of it, Marty!"

"What?"

"Join us over here, please!" McPhee insists.

There's a single-file line at the door, and I'm the only one not in it.

"Come on!" calls Roongrat. "Time to get our pictures taken."

Simon doesn't even notice when I cut in front of him because he's too busy chatting with Parker.

We walk down the hall to the gym, and there's the picture guy all set up and ready. We sit and wait for our names to be called.

Everything moves along just fine until it's Roongrat's turn. He takes forever because this is very serious business to him.

He tries out his expressions.

HAPPY

SERIOUS

FRIENDLY

PENSIVE

EXCITED

BROODING

VULNERABLE

DETERMINED

FLIRTY

Now I wonder what my expression should be when it's my turn.

I decide I want to look artistic.

I try to remember some of the self-portraits that famous artists have painted. What were their facial expressions?

Unfortunately, the only self-portrait I can think of at the moment is Magritte's.

And I didn't bring any apples.

Suddenly, my shoulder hurts.

Simon! Figures! Is it any wonder I loathe the guy?

"It's your turn, idiot!" Simon says. "The picture guy's calling you!"

"LAST CALL FOR PANTS! MARTY PANTS!"

So he is. I hurry over to the stool.

"Hey, howya doin', chief? Nice day. Turn your body. Not that much. Face this way. You like sports? Put your hands like this. Try to act normal."

The picture guy always talks too much.

"Really dressed up for the occasion, didn't cha, chief?" he says.

"This is pretty much how I always look," I say.

"I have a cat," I tell him.

"So do I, but I'm not covered in fur."

"Maybe your cat doesn't love you," I explain.

"Okay, say 'CHEESE,' chief!" he tells me.

I decide not to.

"If you don't like cheese, say 'Bumblebees squeeze breezy fleas and sneeze on their sleazy knees!'"

He's trying to make me smile, but I don't find him very amusing. And I'm not going to force it.

There's nothing worse than a fake smile.

The Mona Lisa faked a smile, and that's all people talk about.

I want to look intense. I want to look like I'm having deep thoughts about something important.

Like art.

Or the meaning of life.

Or the fact that my nose is itchy.

"NEXT! SIMON CARDIGAN!"

"Hey!" I say.

"What's the problem, chief?"

"I wasn't ready!" I tell him.

"Relax, chief," he says. "You'll get a bunch of photos to choose from. I'm behind schedule, so move along, chief."

"But . . ."

"You heard the man," Simon says. "Move along. It's my turn now!"

"But . . ."

"Listen to your friend, chief. He seems like a smart young fella."

"He's the school artist!" Roongrat chimes in.

"Excellent!" the picture guy says. "Move out of the way, chief, so the school Rembrandt can be immortalized!"

GRRRRR

CHAPTER 17
lunch bites

I missed breakfast, so I practically eat my burger in one bite. It hits the spot, but my culinary moment is quickly ruined.

Why is Simon sitting at this table anyway? It's usually just Parker, Roongrat, and me.

Apparently, Simon wants to chat with Parker. I bet she's just as annoyed as I am but acting polite.

Roongrat, on the other hand, is a total Simon fanboy.

"Simon may be the greatest artist of our generation," Roongrat says, significantly louder than he usually talks.

I need to get him off this subject before I lose my lunch.

"Hey, Roongrat," I say. "Sure hope there's no werewolf meat in these burgers!"

"Come again, Marty?" Roongrat can be slow.

So I remind him.

"You told me they found werewolf DNA in burgers, remember? Just this morning? On the way to school?"

A joke isn't funny if you have to explain it.

"Did I say that?" Roongrat asks.

"You sure did, Roonie."

"That's not right. I must have misremembered my true facts."

"You mis-what?"

"I know. It's unusual for me to verbally express some-thing that's less than one hundred percent accurate," Roongrat goes on. "What I meant to convey earlier was that they found dragon DNA in hamburger meat, not werewolf DNA."

What? A werewolf is nothing like a dragon!

"Wait," I say. "So, your opinion on werewolves is . . ."

"I hereby mentally determine they cannot exist," Roongrat says. "If one really ponders it, the uncommon-ality of a moon reaction situation could not overcome the earthly based distance . . ."

I don't hear the rest of his explanation. All I know is if Roongrat thinks werewolves don't exist, that means they totally *do*!

This changes everything!

I reach into my pocket and take out the ripped pieces of the list.

"Doing a puzzle?" asks Roongrat. "The first puzzle was invented by a security guard who accidentally knocked over a monkey skeleton. It's a fact."

Luckily, I have all the pieces and quickly reassemble the list.

There they are, The 12 Werewolf Symptoms.

I uncap my marker and think back to what happened to me in school today.

5. RIPPED CLOTHES ✓

6. AGGRESSION ✓

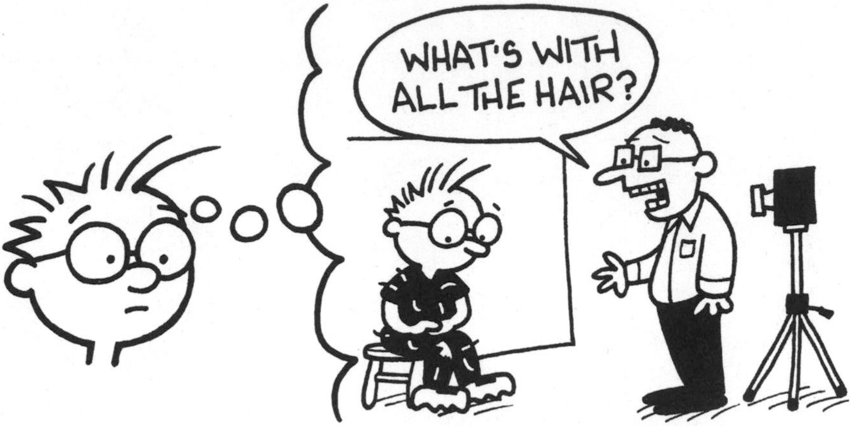
WHAT'S WITH ALL THE HAIR?

7. HAIRINESS ✓

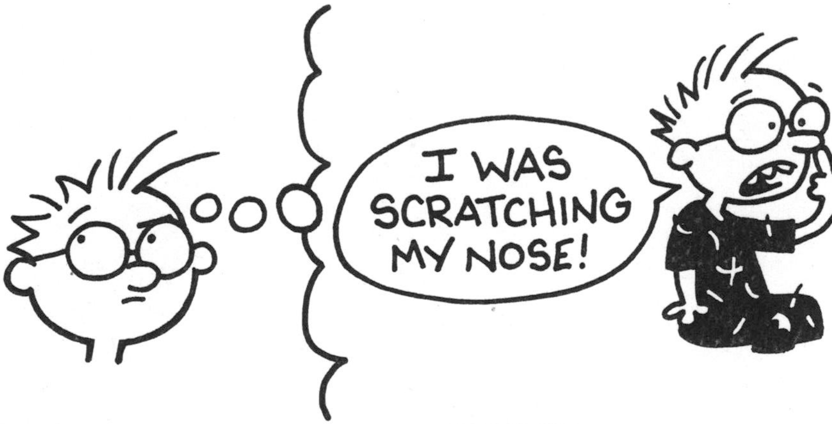
I WAS SCRATCHING MY NOSE!

8. FLEAS ✓

9. GROWLING ✓

10. CRAVING FOR MEAT ✓

I can't believe this! There are only TWO symptoms left!

11. DROOLING

12. SUPERHUMAN STRENGTH

I take a sip of milk, and a bit drips off my lips.

11. DROOLING ✓

It's down to the wire now. I have 11 of The 12 Werewolf Symptoms!

I stare at the list for what feels like forever. Can it be?

There's a tap on my shoulder. It's Ms. Ortiz. "Marty, time to get back to class."

CHAPTER 18

hulks mash

"They're huge!" Simon says.

He's right. The other players are enormous. They certainly picked the right team name.

Our soccer coach is Simon's dad. Coach Cardigan calls us together for a pep talk. "They look big, but we have something they don't!"

"Fear?" asks Carlos.

"NO! THE EYE OF THE LEOPARD!" yells Coach. "We can BEAT these guys if we all give ONE HUNDRED AND SEVENTEEN PERCENT!" I don't think anyone believes that. We haven't had a victory all season, and it doesn't look like we're going to start now.

But sometimes you have to play even though the odds are against you.

The game gets under way, and, as it turns out, not only do they look like hulks, they play like hulks. Our team is getting mashed like potatoes.

"Come on, ref!" Coach Cardigan complains. "Use your EYES! Call penalties on these guys!"

But it doesn't seem to do any good.

I always thought Simon's dad was tough, but the coach of the other team is the meanest, toughest guy I've ever seen.

The game goes on, and our team is getting beaten pretty badly—on the scoreboard and everywhere else.

	SCORE	BRUISES
HULKS	9	0
ANEMONES	0	99

The only good thing I have to report is Coach Cardigan hasn't put me in the game yet.

"TIME OUT!" yells Coach.

Our team huddles up, and I hear moans and groans. "We're not out of it yet!" Coach tells us. "If we can score ONE GOAL, their confidence will be SHATTERED! We can RALLY and TAKE IT TO 'EM!"

"Coach," Roongrat says, "my scapula is agitated."

"Sit out, Roonie. Marty, you're goalkeeper now."

"What? Me? But . . ."

"Okay, team, let me HEAR you!" Coach commands. "ONE, TWO, THREE!"

"That's the spirit! Now give ONE HUNDRED AND SEVENTEEN AND A HALF PERCENT!"

I reluctantly stand in front of the goal. It's not my best position. I stink at it, actually.

But maybe it's safer here than out on the battlefield. Simon inbounds the ball to Carlos, but Hulk #34 bumps into him and kicks the ball to Hulk #12 who heads the ball to Hulk #33 who knees it to Hulk #4 who kicks it at our goal.

My reflexes are sharp, though, and I make an amazing save.

The ball deflects off me, hits a tree, bounces off the top of the fence, bangs into a No Parking sign, then collides with a speeding car.

The ball zooms back onto the field and hits one more hard object.

The Hulks' coach staggers for a few steps, then falls on his back.

He lies there motionless, and everyone is silent. After a few seconds, he rolls onto his stomach and slowly gets onto his hands and knees.

No one makes a sound.

He shakes his head, manages to get to his feet, and walks unsteadily toward the ref.

Then the silence is broken.

Let's just say, those weren't his exact words. "UNSPORTSMANLIKE CONDUCT!" the ref yells. "RED TEAM FORFEITS! BLUE TEAM WINS!"

Blue team? That's us! Our first victory of the season!

To celebrate, Coach takes us to get pizza and ice cream. But I can't fully enjoy the moment.

When I get home, I grab my list.

There's no other way to put it. I knocked out the toughest guy around.

12. SUPERHUMAN STRENGTH ✓

reading is fundamental

I have all of The 12 Werewolf Symptoms. This proves it.

I'm a werewolf!

And I'm the only one who knows it.

Well, not the only one. My sister knows it. And Jerome seems to know it, too.

He no longer sleeps on my head at night. He's been spending a lot of his time under my bed.

Animals can sense things.

He doesn't want to become mincemeat the night I transform into a vicious monster.

Smart cat. Save yourself.

Now, how do I save everyone else?

Maybe it's time to admit to Erica that I read part of her diary and figured out I'm a werewolf.

She'll probably know what I should do.

I head downstairs to face her. Luckily, she's not doing anything important.

"Erica," I say. "About your diary . . ."

"Do you have it, Marty? If you do, I'll cause you a WORLD OF PAIN!"

"I assure you that I do not have your diary," I say honestly. "Just wanted to wish you good luck finding it."

I back away slowly and conclude that discussing this with Erica is a bad idea.

Then I hear a noise behind me. Jerome is sharpening his claws.

And there on the couch is the werewolf novel Erica was reading. That book must contain information on how to cure werewolfism!

I plop down on the couch and skim through the pages. It seems to be full of kissing.

That's not helpful.

Then I finally find something.

There's one sentence that mentions the main weakness of werewolves: "A werewolf is vulnerable to a silver bullet."

Seems drastic.

There must be a better way to undo becoming a were-wolf. I can think of another book that might contain helpful information.

And I know where to look for it.

CHAPTER 20

trash talk

Erica's diary of secrets is somewhere in the town dump. How hard could it be to locate a little book in mountains of garbage?

Let's find out.

I'll recruit my friends, and we can cover a lot of ground. Or rather, cover a lot of trash.

We'll be the D-Team!*

THE D-TEAM

* It stands for the Diary Team. Or the Dump Team. I can't decide.

I explain the important mission to Roongrat, but for some reason he seems to be unavailable.

The D-Team just got smaller.

Now it becomes crucial that Parker agrees to help. How can I convince her to do something this disgusting?

I need to phrase it correctly.

"Parker," I say. "Want to search through some filthy, rotting garbage with me?"

Awesome!

Everything is set. We'll go right after school. But I run into a roadblock.

"Remember to turn in your homework, everyone," McPhee the Roadblock says. "Or you'll get a big, fat zero."

Homework?

CHAPTER 21

you say you want a revolution

As long as I hand in *something*, McPhee won't give me a zero.

I pull a random piece of paper out of my notebook and write "THE AMERICAN REVOLUTION" across the top.

THE AMERICAN REVOLUTION

by Marty Pants

① DISGUISE MYSELF AS MY DAD.

② GO TO THE BANK AND WITHDRAW THOUSANDS OF DOLLARS.

③ GO TO THE ROOF AND THROW THE BILLS OFF THE ROOF.

ERICA WILL THINK IT'S RAINING COLD, HARD CASH!

④ WHEN SHE RUNS OUTSIDE, LOCK THE DOOR BEHIND HER.

"Let me take that for you," I generously tell Roongrat as I grab his homework and place it on top of mine. I hand them both in to McPhee.

Looks like I got away with it. When the bell rings, I immediately zip to the door.

"Marty," McPhee says right before I can escape. "Come up here, please."

Gurk!

"What's this supposed to be?" he asks as he holds up my paper.

"My report on the American Revolution," I say.

"How does this relate to the American Revolution?"

"It was revolutionary of me to hand that in," I tell him. "Alexander Hamilton would approve."

"Detention, Marty."

"What? I don't have the time! A person and a pile of garbage are waiting for me!"

"Do you even know who Alexander Hamilton is?"

I remember Erica saying random things about history all week, so I give it a shot.

"He founded the Federalist Party, which pushed for a strong federal government," I say. "He was the first secretary of the Treasury, created America's financial system, and was one of the most important advisors to George Washington."

"Lucky guess," McPhee says. "What about James Madison?"

"He's known as the 'Father of the Constitution' and wrote the Bill of Rights and was the fourth president."

"Um . . ." McPhee says. He appears to be looking all of that up on his computer.

"And by the way, the American Revolutionary War was from 1775–1783," I say.

McPhee looks astonished.

I probably do, too.

"I'm impressed, Marty," he admits. "You really studied!"

"Sure, that's exactly what I did. Can I go now? Can that count as my homework?"

"I'll let you off the hook this time, but next time, write it down!"

"Thanks, Mr. McPhee! You're the best! Well, you're not really the best, per se. Let's just say . . ."

"Good-bye, Marty."

"Bye, Mr. McPhee!"

I hightail it out of there before Parker thinks I stood her up!

CHAPTER 22

pump it up

The dump is a good distance away, so I'll have to bike it. I can't use my superhuman speed without arousing suspicion.

I get home but can't find my bike anywhere!

I ask Erica if she's seen it, but she's even less help than usual.

THURGOOD MARSHALL...
SHIRLEY CHISHOLM...
JACKIE ROBINSON...

Oh yeah. My bike is still at Parker's!

I rush over and find it right where I left it. But it has a flat.

I forgot about that.

Before I can figure out what to do, there's an ominous voice behind me. "I was wondering what boy that bike belonged to."

Uh-oh.

"Hi there, Mr. Fedora."

"Follow me, Marty."

Sigh.

I knew it would eventually come to this. Parker's dad is going to make me into a piece of high-quality furniture.

Maybe this is best for society. He'll turn me into a nightstand before I turn into a night stalker.

For the good of mankind, I accept my fate and follow Mr. Fedora to the front of the garage.

I'll never get to grow up. I'll never become a famous artist. I'll never become a father.

But there's still a chance I'll become a grandfather.

Mr. Fedora opens the garage door, gets an air pump, and inflates the tire.

"There you go, Marty. It was just a little low."

"Thanks, Mr. Fedora!"

"Are you here looking for Parker?" he asks me. I don't answer. This might be a trick question.

"Hey, Marty!" Parker calls down from a nearby tree.

"Hey, Parker!" I say. "You ready?"

"Dad! I'm going bike riding."

"Okay, have fun," Mr. Fedora says. "But be back for dinner."

Then I hear a familiar voice behind me. "Hello, Marty." It's Roongrat.

"I decided to attend after all," he says. "I heard Simon will be there."

"You heard wrong," I say. "But welcome to the team, Roonie."

Then I hear *another* familiar voice. "Hey, Parker!"

Simon? What's that monkey washer doing here?!

"Hope you don't mind, Marty," Parker says as she climbs down from the tree. "I invited Simon."

MIND? OF COURSE, I MIND! I say loudly inside my head.

"Mind? Why would I mind?" I say calmly out of my mouth.

the d-team

Once I get over the shock of that monkey-washing Simon joining us, I decide that having four people on the D-Team is a good thing after all.

THE D-TEAM

When we arrive at the dump, there's a hole in the fence, so it's easy to sneak in. I guess no one bothered to fix it because most normal people don't want to sneak into a dump.

One thing's clear, though. This place stinks!

I wonder if my enhanced canine sense of smell makes it worse for me than the others.

Or maybe it makes it better. If memory serves me correctly, canines *like* the smell of stinky things.

I hand out the gloves and bandannas that I borrowed from my mom's gardening supplies. Luckily, I brought enough.

Then the D-Team spreads out.

It soon occurs to me that Simon hasn't insulted me once since we started. And he seems surprisingly motivated.

I bet it's because he has a crush on my sister and wants to see if he's mentioned in her diary.*

Meanwhile, Roongrat keeps getting distracted.

* Erica doesn't know Simon exists, but I see no reason to bring that up to him right now.

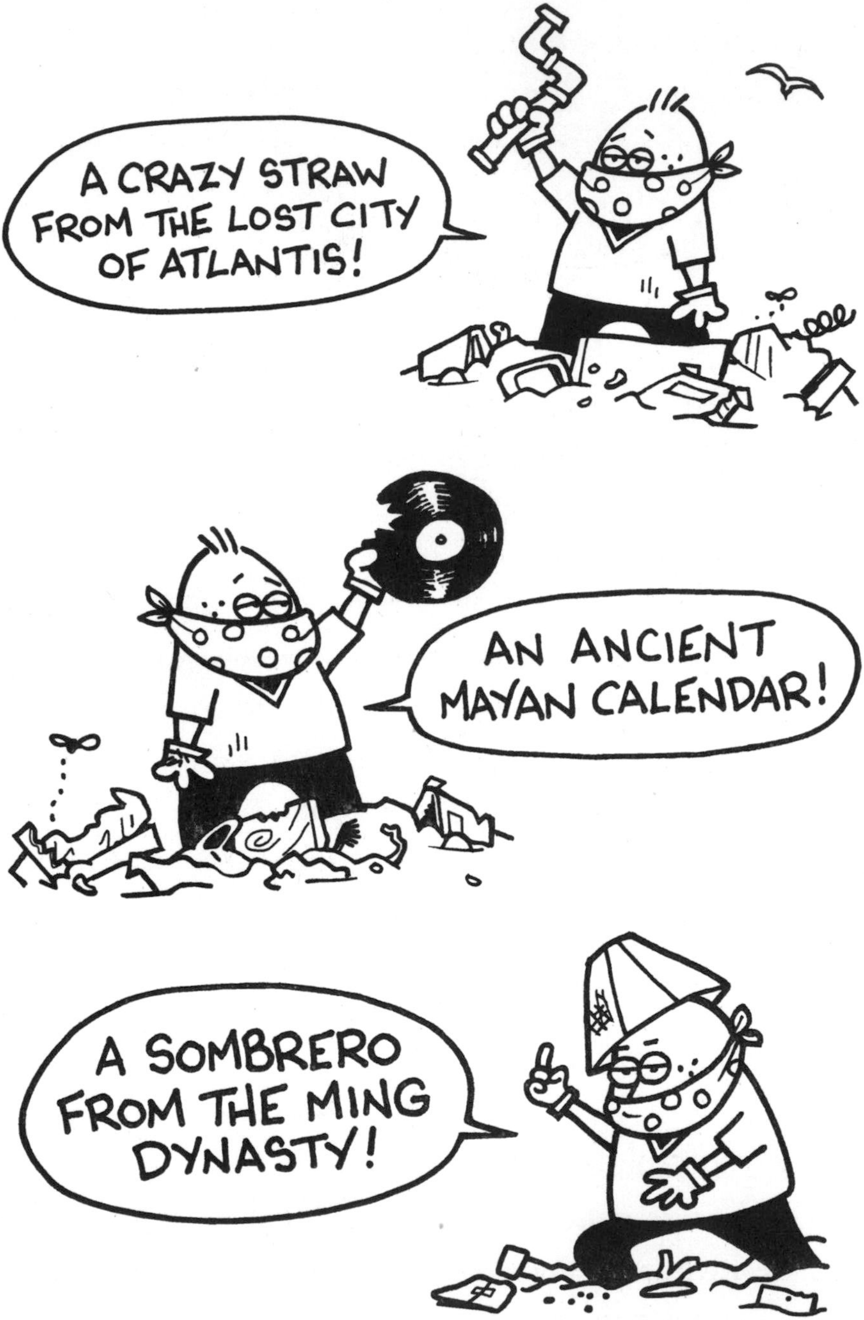
A CRAZY STRAW FROM THE LOST CITY OF ATLANTIS!
AN ANCIENT MAYAN CALENDAR!
A SOMBRERO FROM THE MING DYNASTY!

Parker gets sidetracked, too.

As for me, I stay completely focused on looking for the diary.

That is, until I find a Twinkie still in the wrapper. You really work up an appetite searching through garbage.

I sit on an old tire and unwrap the spongy treat, but before I can take a bite, it's snatched from my hand.

"DEWEEEEEEY!" yells Parker.

She chases him with the crate, but Dewey zigs and zags. There are a zillion hiding places here, and soon that pooch is nowhere to be found.

"Poor dog," Parker says. "He eats garbage that he finds in the dump."

I look at the empty wrapper in my hand. "Yeah," I say. "Can't imagine doing that."

Eventually, Simon begins to lose his enthusiasm and reverts back to his usual self.

SMELLS LIKE YOUR ART, MARTY!

Before I have a chance to kick him off the D-Team, Simon quits on his own.

Roongrat follows suit. Then Parker!

The D-Team falls like dominoes!*

"Had a blast, Marty," Parker says, "but I have to get home for dinner. Sorry we couldn't find your sister's diary, but it was a long shot anyway."

"Thanks for trying," I say.

* I guess it's now the Domino Team.

I offer to carry the dog crate to Parker's bike and tie it to the back, but when I try to pick it up, it's heavier than I expected. I peek inside.

It's Dewey!
"Parker!" I say. "We caught Dewey!"
The door flies open.

Once the shock wears off and I get up off my butt, I apologize to Parker for getting her hopes up.

"That's okay," she says. "I'll catch him one day!"

Everyone else heads home, and that means the D-Team is down to just me.

And that's the moment I discover something: walking around in garbage alone isn't as much fun.

Time to face the music. The mission was a failure. The diary is gone forever, and I'll never know if it held any important antiwerewolf secrets.

But the day wasn't a total loss. I did find something useful.

On the way home, I stop at the store to buy a candy bar. I can tell people are acting weird around me.

Seems the public is starting to sense that I'm becoming a monster.

CHAPTER 24

crazy ache

I wake up with a toothache.

It must be my fangs growing in. My dad thinks it's a cavity. "Seems far-fetched," I say.

"Marty, you ate thirty bars of candy."

"WHAT?" yells my mom. She was on a business trip at the time, and this is news to her.

"You're going to the dentist!" she insists.

My mom has a way of getting appointments right away.

I have to go to Dr. Distal's office straight after school.

I loathe the idea. I've never enjoyed having dentistry inflicted on me.

But now that I think about it, this could be the solution I'm looking for!

I can instruct the dentist to pull out all my teeth. That way, when I turn into a werewolf, I'll be harmless!

Yes. That makes perfect sense. Unlike my sister.

She hasn't been making much sense at all lately. She's completely consumed with fear about what her little brother is about to become, and she's talking crazy gibberish.

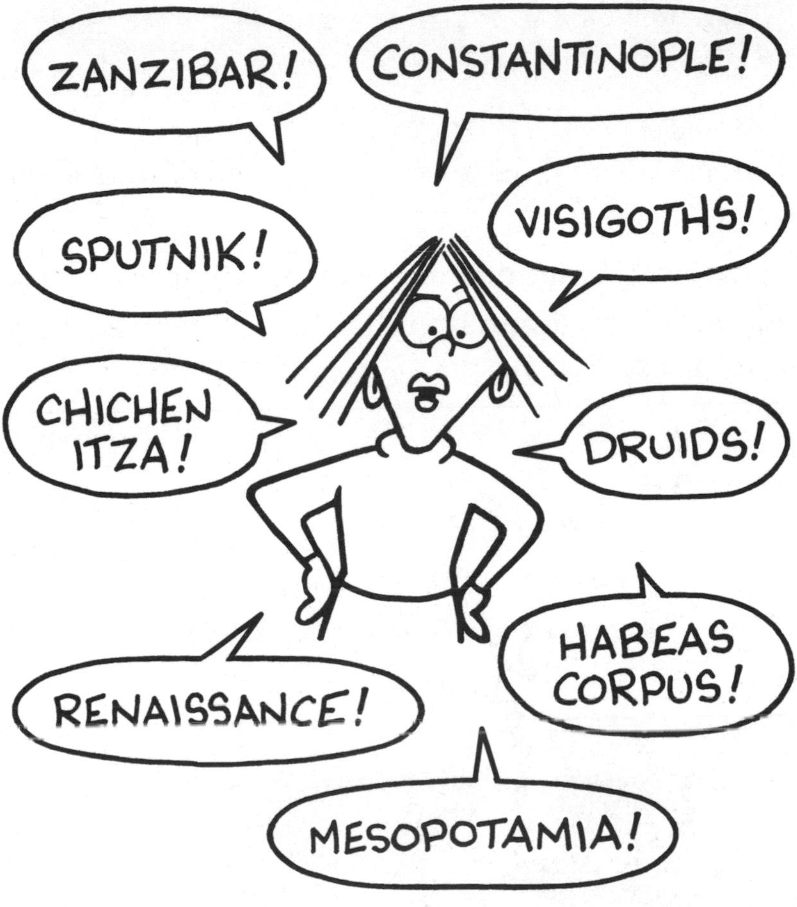
ZANZIBAR!
CONSTANTINOPLE!
SPUTNIK!
VISIGOTHS!
CHICHEN ITZA!
DRUIDS!
RENAISSANCE!
HABEAS CORPUS!
MESOPOTAMIA!

CHAPTER 25

gut feeling

How many days before I turn into a werewolf? It's about time I checked.

"Parker," I ask casually, "do you know when the next full moon is?"

"Saturday," she says.

"You didn't even have to look it up?"

"Nope," she says. "That's when the Full Moon Festival is."

"The what?"

Parker hands me a flyer.

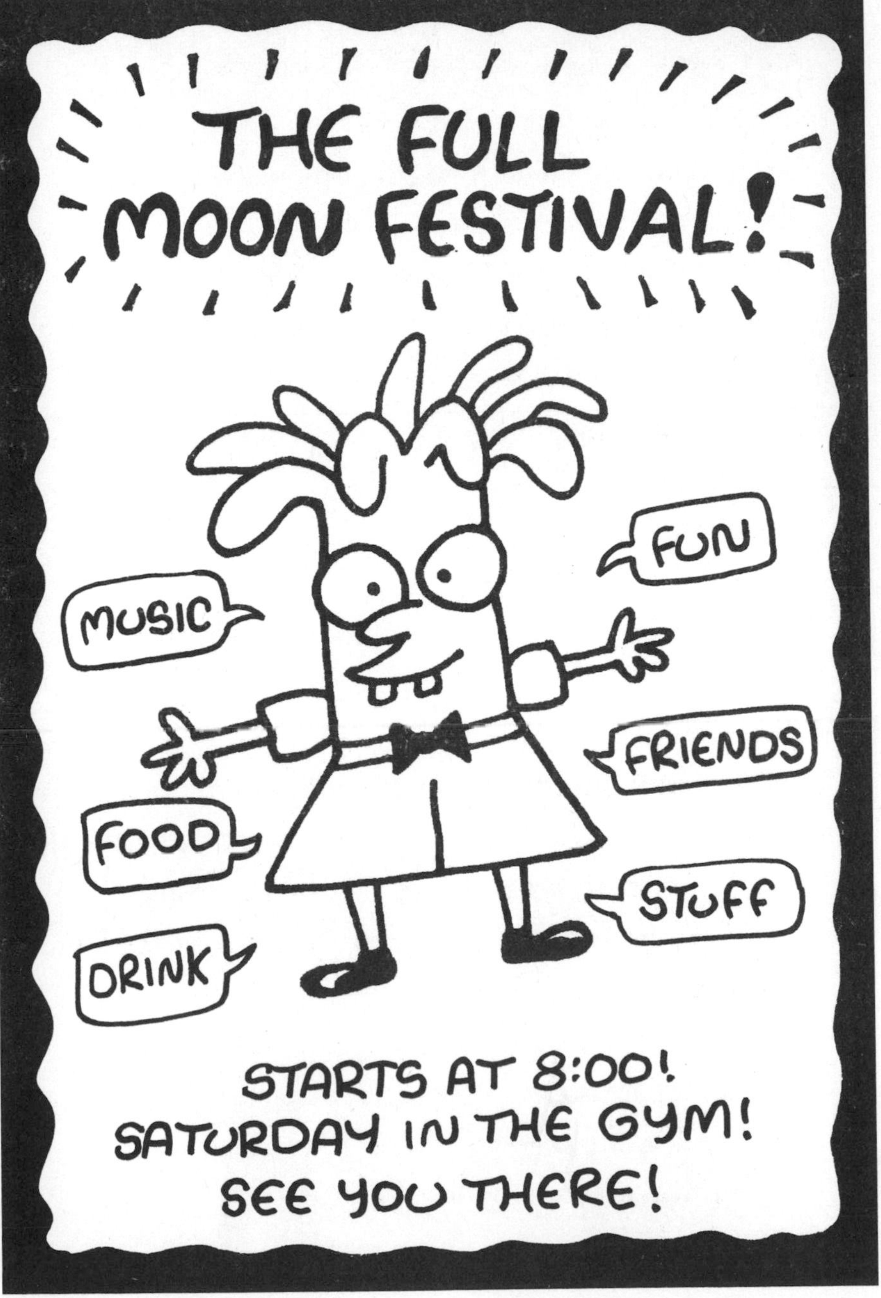
THE FULL MOON FESTIVAL!
MUSIC
FUN
FRIENDS
FOOD
STUFF
DRINK
STARTS AT 8:00!
SATURDAY IN THE GYM!
SEE YOU THERE!

This is the dumbest flyer I've ever seen.

"Didn't Simon give you one?" she asks.

"Nope."

"Well, there are plenty hanging up on the walls."

I look around. She's right.

"Want to go with me?" Parker says with a big smile.

"Go with you?" I ask.

"Yes."

"You and me together?"

"Together."

"To an event."

"Right."

"You and me going to an event together?"

"You got it!"

I think she's asking me out.

But she's still under the impression that I'm not a were-wolf. I haven't told her I actually *AM* a werewolf after all. Maybe it's better this way. It's my burden to bear.

And I loathe the idea of Parker being scared of me.

"No, thank you," I say.

"No?"

"No," I repeat.

"You don't want to go with me?"

"I don't think it's a good idea, Parker."

"Oh. Okay then."

Parker looks hurt, but she's certainly not as hurt as she'd be if I'd said yes. The last place I should be during a full moon is a gymnasium full of people!

Especially if one of those people is Parker.

She walks away, devastated I'm sure.

She gets over it quickly, though, because I hear her laughing.

"Parker, want to go to the Full Moon Festival with me?" I overhear Simon say.

"Let me think about it," Parker answers. She glances over at me. I look away.

"I thought about it," she says to Simon. "I'll go!"

"Great! My dad can drive us!"

"Great!" Parker says as she heads off to class.

Simon looks over at me, then proceeds to do his annoying victory dance.

This time with lyrics.

Meanwhile, my chest is starting to hurt. I wonder if this is another symptom of becoming a werewolf.

toothiness

"Take them all out," I tell Dr. Distal.

"No need for that," she says. "I'll just fill that nasty cavity."

"I'm the customer," I remind her.

"You sure are," she replies. "And I'll do my best to make you happy."

"That's what I like to hear."

She looks inside my mouth.

"How much candy do you eat, Marty?"

"The recommended daily amount," I say.

"How about you cut down a little?"

"I guess I'll have to," I say. "It'll be hard to eat candy without any teeth."

"My point exactly," she says.

Dr. Distal talks a big game, but when I leave her office, I check my reflection in the grocery store window.

I still have all my teeth!

She put plenty of dangerous-looking instruments in my mouth, but all she ultimately did was give me one big filling.

Then, right before my eyes, I see my face begin to change.

I'm transforming! Already?!

Wait. That's not a reflection … there's an actual canine on the other side of the glass.

Dewey!

The store employees chase him around and bump into each other. Dewey even manages to grab a few snacks while he dodges everyone.

He's very entertaining. I can see why Parker likes him so much.

A woman enters the store, and Dewey takes the opportunity to escape.

He darts left, right, left, then behind the building. I think about chasing him, but he's too crafty.

When I get home, my mom is packing for another business trip.

"How'd it go at the dentist?" she asks.

"Wi wink ik wenk wine bu wi shill hab aw my deef," I say, waiting for the numbness to wear off.

CHAPTER 27

game on

The full moon is only two days away!

I've been brainstorming all week but haven't come up with a solution.

I have to find a way to stop myself from transforming!

I invite Roongrat to play video games after school.

I need a break to clear my head.

He brings a new game he's dying to try out.

As you may have guessed from the title, the object of the game is to eat the dragon before it eats you.

"How come you're not going to the Full Moon Festival?" Roongrat asks. "Everyone's going. Even Jasmine. And Jasmine doesn't go to anything."

I DON'T GO TO ANYTHING.

"Health reasons," I say.

"Simon is going with Parker, you know."

"I'm well aware of that!"

"It's due to Simon's artistic abilities," Roongrat says. "It's a fact. His influential art skills convinced everyone to attend."

"Not me!" I remind him.

"Simon's talent stems from his eyelids," Roongrat adds. "Droopy eyelids indicate an advanced creativity center in the cerebellum section of the brain matter. It's a fact."

Ugh. I can't listen to this anymore.

"Let's play *Dragon Eater*!" I say.

It turns out my predatory instincts are an advantage in this game. I'm doing very well. In fact, I'm flying through the levels!

"Have you played this before, Marty?" Roongrat asks.

"No. I guess I'm just a natural."

I did it! I ate the entire dragon!

There's a *burp* sound effect, then another screen pops up.

"Hey, you ate me!" Roongrat whines.

"Sorry. I didn't even know that was possible."

"Well, don't do it again!"

"Unfortunately, Roonie, that's a promise I can't make."

Roongrat grabs his game and heads home in a huff. I kick back in my beanbag of solitude and think.

It won't be safe for anyone to go out during the full moon. I need to prevent all the kids from going to the Full Moon Festival.

But how?

What I need is another epiphany.

Bang. Got one.

CHAPTER 28
flyer away

Throughout history, great art has always had a way of changing minds.

That means all I have to do is make a flyer that's superior to Simon's and convince Parker to stay home! I mean, convince everyone to stay home!

It's so simple—why didn't I think of this before? Dueling flyers.

May the best flyer win. (Mine, of course.)

Simon's flyer is so lame that this should be a cakewalk.

I grab a clean sheet of paper and get to work.

After a couple of hours, I add the finishing touches. It's to the point, but is it powerful enough to cancel out Simon's flyer?

Is it a mind changer?

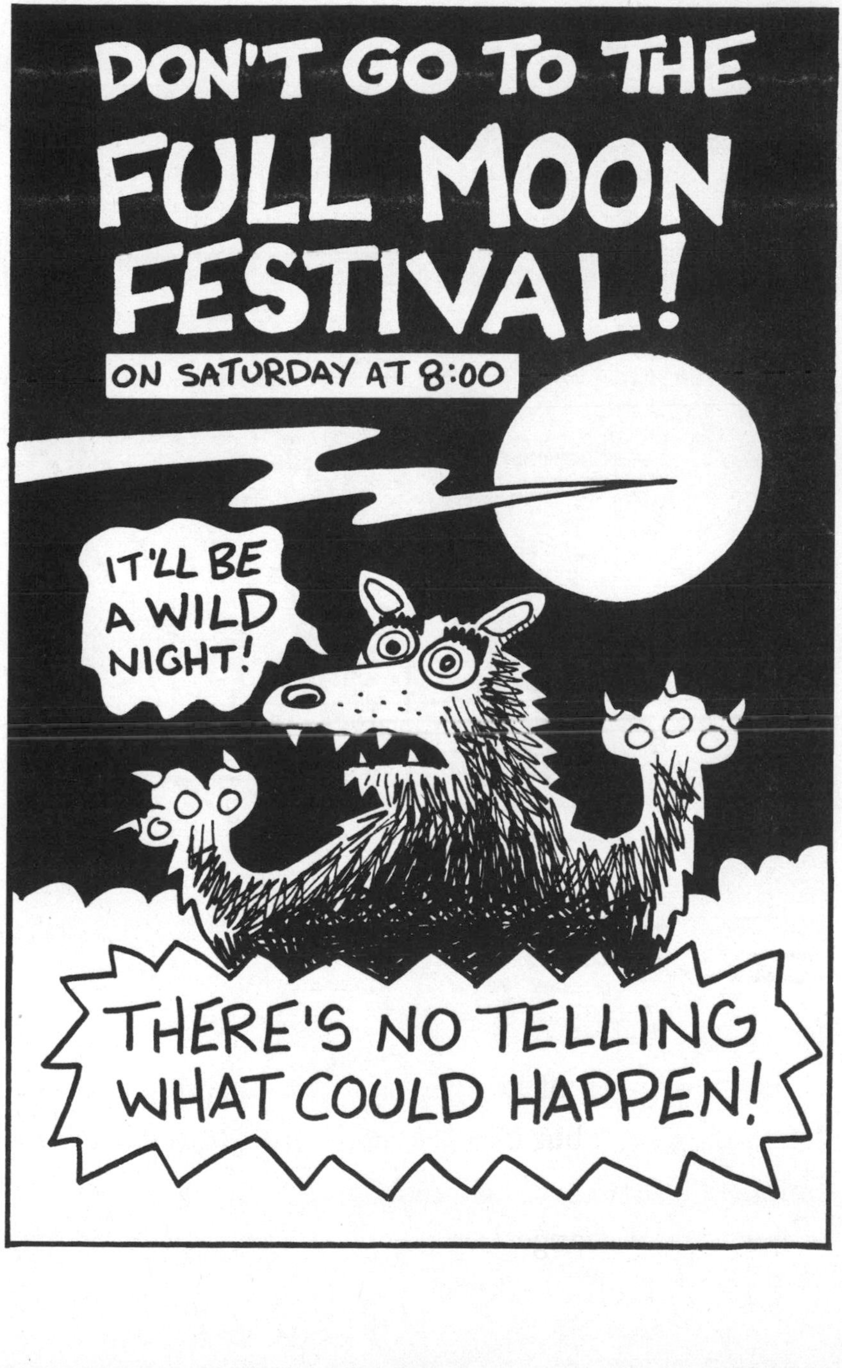
DON'T GO TO THE
FULL MOON
FESTIVAL!
ON SATURDAY AT 8:00
IT'LL BE A WILD NIGHT!
THERE'S NO TELLING WHAT COULD HAPPEN!

I decide it's awesome, but now I worry it gives away too much.

I don't want to give anyone any clues that I'm about to become a crazed werewolf. That could cause a nationwide panic.

I need a second opinion. My door flies open.

"Perfect timing!" I say. "Come here and tell me what you think. I trust your opinion."

Jerome obediently leaps over to me. "What do you think of this, little buddy?"

Jerome rolls around on my flyer, nibbles the corner, does a somersault, lands in my lap, and rubs against my face, purring.

That's what I call a rave review!

Sure, one might assume Jerome's wacky behavior is due to the catnip that's hidden in Erica's backpack, but I can tell he's under the influence of something even more powerful.

Brilliant art.

CHAPTER 29

should you stay or should you go

I get to school early and head straight to the office.

"Ms. Ortiz, can I make some copies?"

"Sure, Marty! What do you have there?"

"A flyer for the Full Moon Festival," I reply honestly.

"Oooooh, exciting! Can I see?"

"I want it to be a surprise!" I say, just as honestly.

"Of course, Marty. The copier's right there."

Ms. Ortiz may be the only adult at the school who regularly encourages my artistic abilities. I hope I don't get her in trouble!

I work fast and manage to get out of the office right before Principal Cricklewood shows up.

On the way to class, I run into Parker in the hall.

"Marty," she says. "Simon asked me to go to the Full Moon Festival with him."

"Yes, I'm very aware!"

"I'm having second thoughts, though. What do you think I should do?"

What a perfect setup. I hand her one of my persuasive flyers.

Parker reads it, obviously appreciating the artistic way the message is being conveyed.

She looks back up at me.

"Great flyer, Marty," she says. "You just changed my mind."

Yes! Success!*

Throughout the day, I hand out the flyers and hang them in the hall next to Simon's flyers.

I get maximum coverage.

---

* My art is so powerful, I must remember to use it for good, never evil.

Kids come up to me throughout the day to compliment my antifestival flyer.

But not Simon. He knows I got the best of him. When the full moon comes, all the kids will remain safe in their homes while I am out doing dangerous werewolf stuff.

I want everyone to be safe. Except maybe Simon.

I don't really mind if he wanders out tomorrow night.

Before I leave class, McPhee calls me to his desk. "Principal Cricklewood wants to see you in her office, Marty."

Uh-oh. I knew this was coming.

She saw my flyer and is upset I convinced everyone to avoid the Full Moon Festival.

Principal Cricklewood isn't exactly a fan of my work.

It all started a couple of years ago when I was called into her office for an art-related misunderstanding.

I got caught doodling on my desk during a particularly boring class.

I remember that Cricklewood sat me down and gave me a major lecture. It was longer than most movies I've seen. Before she was finished, she had to leave her office for some minor emergency.

I got bored waiting for her to come back, so, naturally, I looked around for some paper to draw on.

Unfortunately, my elbow hit her deceptively labeled mug.

Coffee spilled all over her family picture!

I grabbed some tissues and wiped it off, but for some reason, there was no protective glass over the photo. As a result, things didn't go as expected.

I managed to fix everything by the time Cricklewood came back, but she showed me absolutely no appreciation whatsoever.

Apparently, some people have no respect for quality art.

So, here I am on my way to get lectured by Cricklewood once again.

When I arrive at the office, Ms. Ortiz gives me the thumbs-up.

Cricklewood gives me a smile. This seems like a trick.

"I just want to say you did a superb job on the flyers for the Full Moon Festival!" the person who looks like Principal Cricklewood says to me.

"I did?" I say, more than a little confused.

"You really showed your school spirit, Marty! I'm so proud of you!"

"Thanks?" I say.

I leave the office unsure of what just happened. I walk over to one of the flyers posted on the wall.

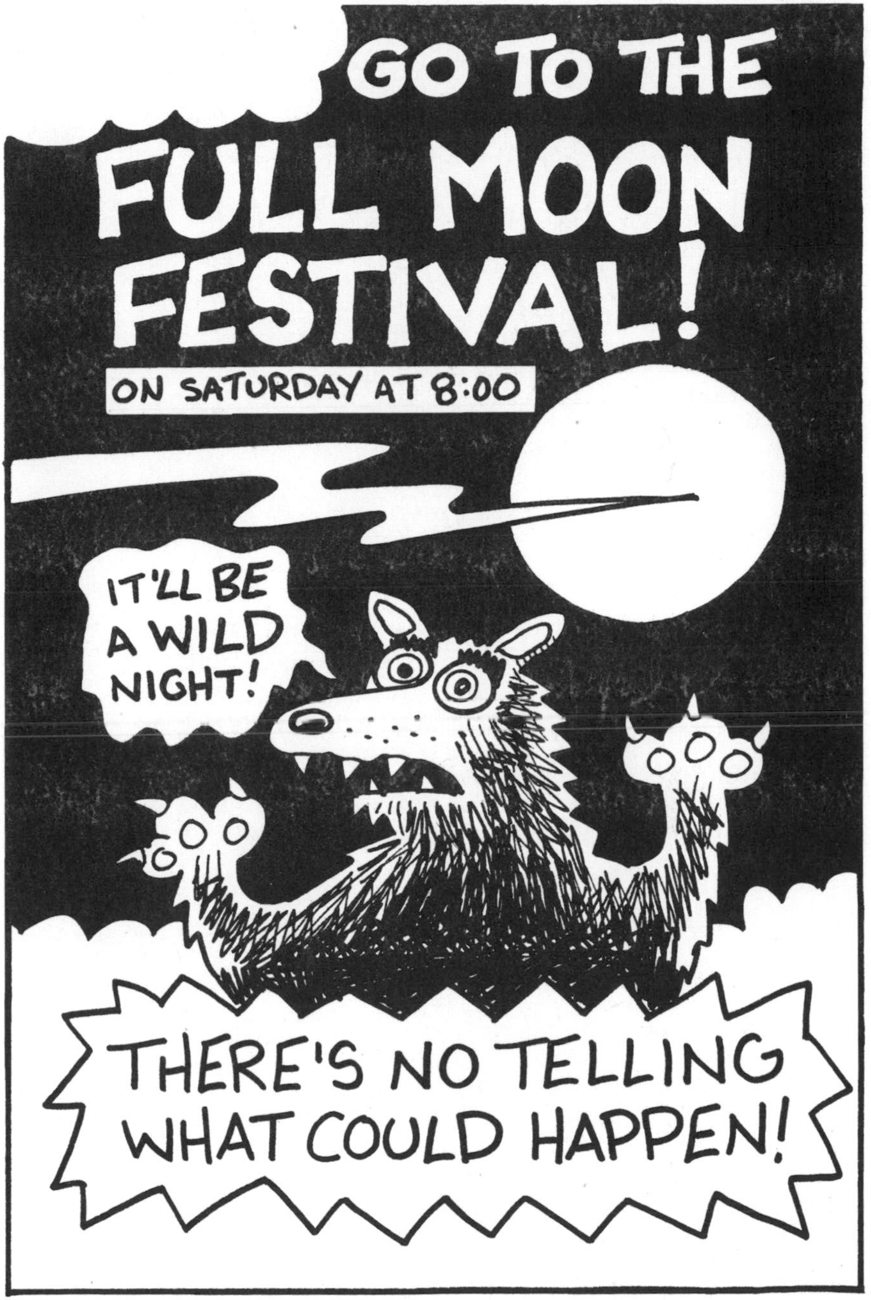
GO TO THE
FULL MOON
FESTIVAL!
ON SATURDAY AT 8:00
IT'LL BE A WILD NIGHT!
THERE'S NO TELLING WHAT COULD HAPPEN!

The *DON'T* is gone!

The *DON'T* was the most important part of the entire message!

What happened to the *DON'T*?

I pull out the original drawing from my backpack, the one I used to make all the copies.

The *DON'T* has been chewed off! How did I not notice this?!

How did this even happen?!

Wait.

I bet I know where that *DON'T* ended up.

CHAPTER 30

bad moon rising

I try to stay calm, but Erica is freaking out.

> HARRIET TUBMAN!
> GENGHIS KHAN!
> MAHATMA GANDHI!
> JOAN OF ARC!
> NAPOLÉON!
> ARISTOTLE!
> SUSAN B. ANTHONY!
> HIAWATHA!

She knows I'll be transforming soon so she's listing all the people she wants to warn.

I can tell my sister hasn't told our mom or dad yet because they are much more relaxed than she is.

I guess Erica realizes news like this would break their hearts.

I need to do something, but I don't know what! And I'm running out of time!

The full moon is *tonight*.

The good news is my family will be safe.

- Jerome will be secure hiding under my bed.
- My mom will be away on another business trip.
- My dad will be with Erica at the History Trivia Contest in another city. They're staying overnight.

Now I understand why Erica signed up for the contest in the first place. She wants everyone to be away when

I become a brutish, bloodthirsty beast.

I'll have returned to fully human form by the time everyone gets back.

I admire her plan. The problem is I'm supposed to sleep over Roongrat's tonight.

That complicates things.

My mom comes downstairs with her suitcase and says her good-byes.

"Good luck in the contest!" she says to Erica.

"Stop destroying the couch!" she says to Jerome.

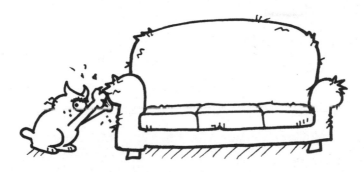

"We need a new couch!" she says to my dad.

"Have fun with Roongrat!" she says to me.

I hug her for a long time and extra tightly. Must be my superhuman strength.

Once she's gone, I ask my dad why I can't stay home by myself for one night. One night!

"We thought it would be better this way," he answers vaguely.

"Worried I'll rip the house apart?" I ask.

"Well, um . . . Erica, let's go!" he says. "Marty, I'll drop you off at Roongrat's."

"I'll bike over," I tell him. "Leave me some dignity."

"Fine. Just remember to lock up when you leave."

"I will," I promise. "And Erica. Try to stay calm. Everything will be all right."

"Thanks, Marty," she says. I see her smile for the first time in a long time.

I give them a thumbs-up as they drive off.

I lock up the house, as promised, and get on my bike.

But I'm not going to Roongrat's.

CHAPTER 31

everybody's got something to hide

I have no money for zoo admission.*

But I do have a plan. I tell the guy at the window I'm doing an article for the school paper.

I'm waved in.

It's like a secret password that gets me into almost anywhere.

I watch the monkeys for a while. They look hungry. I'm not sure if they eat pinecones, but I think they do, so I give them some.

---

* My allowance is still paying for all that expensive fund-raiser candy.

As fun as monkey watching is, it's not why I'm here. I march to the zookeeper's office and knock on the door.

"Come in!"

I obey. And there's the zookeeper.

"Hi," I say. "Marty Pants, school reporter. I have a few questions."

"Hi. Emily Xing, zookeeper. Ask away."

"Do you have any empty cages I could spend the night in?"

"If it were up to me, sure, but they don't allow us to put humans in zoo cages."

"What about werewolves? Can you put werewolves in cages?"

"Depends. Would this werewolf be a werewolf one hundred percent of the time?"

"Well, a human most of the time. That's how werewolf-ism works."

"Again, we're not allowed to keep humans in zoo cages."

"But it would only be for tonight. The night of the full moon. Can't you bend the rules?"

"Too much paperwork."

"But . . ."

"Tell you what. Write your congressional representative. If Congress passes a law allowing us to put humans or partial humans in zoo cages, come back and we'll talk."

"Who's my congressional representative?" I ask.

Zookeeper Xing types on her computer.

"There we go," she says. "Representative Penelope P. Plunket."

She turns the computer to show me the screen. I see a web page with a smiling woman.

Zookeeper Xing gets a phone call and has to leave her office suddenly for a "zoo-mergency."

I notice a Contact Me link on the web page and click it. Then I see a big open space and the words, "Write your message here."

I start typing.

Subject: IMPORTANT!

Dear Congressional Representative Penelope P. Plunket,

I'm going to let you in on a secret. I'm about to turn into a werewolf. If you could pass a law right now giving the zoo permission to lock me in a cage tonight, I'd appreciate it. So would society.

Sincerely,
Marty Pants

My message disappears, and new message pops up immediately.

Congress is so efficient!

> Dear Constituent,
>
> Thank you for your message. As your congressperson, I appreciate hearing from you and will make every effort to respond in a timely manner. Please be patient.
> Your government cares.
>
> > Best regards,
> > Rep. Penelope P. Plunket

Wait a minute. Government?

I've watched a lot of movies, and every time the government finds out people have mysterious superpowers, it's always the same story.

Kidnap them, drag them to a secret military base, and try to make an army of clones!

Then, one way or another, things go wrong. Horribly, horribly wrong!

And I just alerted the government about my super-human powers!

And even included my name! I have to fix this. *Fast!*

I click on Contact Me again.

Subject: EVEN MORE IMPORTANT!

Just kidding! Ha-ha! No need to kidnap me! And Marty Pants isn't even my real name!

Sincerely,
Simon Cardigan

Whew. That was close.

From now on, I'll have to be more careful.

Now what? I need a new plan!

Hold on.

Here it comes.

Wait for it.

An epiphany.

I know exactly who can help me! I walk quickly to the exit.

CHAPTER 32

crime and punishment

"I'm here to see Officer Pickels," I tell the police officer at the front desk.

"What is this concerning?"

"Secret Marty Pants business," I explain.

"You'll have to be more specific," she says.

Fine. If that's the way she wants to play it. "I'm writing an article for the school paper."

In less than a minute, Officer Pickels comes up to meet me. He holds out his hand.

He obviously wants a bribe.

Luckily, he's satisfied with a handshake.

"Hi, Marty. Here for another school project?"

"Officer Pickels, you've got to arrest me."

"For what?"

"I'm going to turn into a, um, do you work for the government?"

"Yes, I do."

"Then I robbed a bank."

"Good grief. In that case, you'll have to go away for a long time, Marty."

"No, forget that. I only need to go away for one night."

"Why is that?"

"It's complicated."

"The jails are not for overnight sleepovers, Marty."

"I'm not expecting a free night in jail," I assure him. "I'll earn it. Maybe we could brainstorm and come up with some crime I could commit. Something less serious than robbing a bank."

"You want me to conspire with you to commit a crime?"

"Yes, that's what I'm doing. Conspiring! Conspiring must be worth a night in jail! Arrest me."

"And this is for school?" Officer Pickels asks.

"No," I say. "I mean, YES! For school!"

"This seems like a strange project."

"I want to write an article for the school paper about spending one night in jail! That's totally the reason I'm here!"

"Well, if you can get your parents and the school to agree to this, I'll consider it."

"I just lied to you, Officer Pickels. This is not for school! Arrest me."

Officer Pickels stares blankly at me for a moment.

"You're an artist, right, Marty?"

"I sure am."

"Is this performance art?"

"What's performance art, Officer Pickels?"

"This weird conversation we're having reminds me of performance art. Are you performing? My wife took me to see some performance art once, and I didn't understand it at all."

"I was as confused then as I am right now," he tells me.

"Is performance art illegal?" I ask hopefully.

"No, but I think it should be."

"Man, I can't get arrested in this town," I say.

"You're a good kid, Marty. Why don't you forget all about this performance art and go make some *real* art?"

"Great idea, Officer Pickels! Thanks for the epiphany!"

CHAPTER 33

the wall

Officer Pickels told me to make art. Excellent advice.

I'll deface a building with graffiti! I know for a fact that'll get me put behind bars.

I have no money for spray paint, but I do have something else with me.

I look for a building to vandalize with my talent.

This will do nicely.

All I need to do is draw something that all the candy people will loathe.

It has to be so offensive, so repugnant, they won't hesitate to call the police on me.

No problem.

Perfect! That will get me thrown in the hoosegow for sure!

I stand there for a while, but no one seems to be paying attention.

I tap on a window for a minute or two, and finally an important-looking man comes outside.

I point to Mr. Candy and say, "I drew that."

"You did?" asks Mr. Important.

"Yup. On purpose, too."

I hold out my wrists so he can make a citizen's arrest.

"Go ahead," I say. "Get the handcuffs."

"Ha-ha! Nice job, kid. That's well drawn and funny!"

"Huh?"

"There's a distinct sense of edginess combined with appealing accessibility."

"But . . ."

He opens the door and calls inside. "Hey, Krystal! Come check this out! Ha-ha!"

Gurk! This is the *one time* I don't want someone to like my art! Of all the rotten luck!

Krystal joins us. "Clever! You're a talented young man!"

I don't have time for this! I grab my bike and pedal away.

As I turn the corner, something darts in front of me.

Dewey! And he's being chased.

Of course! Animal control!

They would know what to do with me. That's their job! They deal with dangerous animals every day!

I wave my arms, and the van pulls over.

"Did you see where that dog went, kid? He's a danger to the community."

"Never mind him. I know a bigger danger," I say.

"You do, kid? Where?"

I pick up an empty candy wrapper from the ground and write my address on it.

"Here. Come by in about an hour, before it gets dark," I tell him.

"Whatever, kid. Right now I need to find that dog. He's a slippery bugger. I've been trying to catch him for almost a month. Know anything about him?"

"Only that he's a good kisser," I say.

The van speeds off.

I feel better now. I found a true professional to handle things.

On my way home, I stop by Parker's house to ask if I can borrow that dog crate she found at the dump.

Her dad answers the door.

"Parker's not here, Marty. She went to the Full Moon Festival with Simon."

Why does everybody keep reminding me?!

"It was your flyer that convinced her to go."

Gurk! Stop it!

"I'm just here to ask if I can borrow Parker's dog crate, Mr. Fedora."

"Parker has a dog crate?"

"Yes."

"Why?"

"I guess she's in love."

"In love?" he asks.

"Head over heels."

"With whom?"

"Dewey. A stray dog," I tell him. "I thought you knew."

"She never mentioned any dog to me."

"Maybe she was afraid to tell you. Scared you'd break her heart. Smash it to little pieces. Crush her hopes and dreams. Cause unspeakable pain and anguish . . ."

"Okay, okay, Marty! You can borrow the crate!"

CHAPTER 34

out of control

I wait in my room for the animal control guy to show up. He better get here soon because I don't know how long this crate will hold me once I transform.

Plus, it's uncomfortable. My legs are cramping. Hopefully, I'll relax when he shoots me with a tranquilizer dart.

No one will be home until tomorrow, so I made sure Jerome won't go hungry.

There's a knock on the door. "COME IN!" I yell.

I should be downstairs. I hope he doesn't have trouble finding me.

"UP HERE!" I yell.

I hear some kind of commotion. Things are getting knocked around. Something just broke.

Is this guy really that much of a klutz?

I rock back and forth and manage to roll the crate off the bed. With a lot of effort, I scoot myself to the top of the stairs.

I look down to the first floor.

What a disaster! Then I catch a glimpse of the animal control guy.

He's struggling with something.

JEROME?!

"STOP!" I scream. "I AM THE DANGER!" I don't think he can hear me.

And the lock on the crate is stuck!

The animal control guy drags Jerome outside. I've got to rescue him!

Time to use superhuman strength.

I start shaking and rattling and pretty soon I'm rolling down the stairs.

CRASHBOOMBANG!

FLUMP!

I'm free!

Now to use my superhuman speed to catch the van!

Wait.

It's getting dark.

I could transform into a beast at any moment!

If I'm going to run around outside, I need a way to protect society from my dangerousness.

But how?

I look around for a solution.

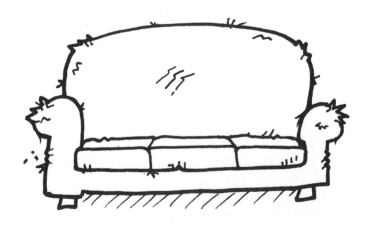

The couch.

Jerome's been clawing it for years, and it's held up just fine.

I grab the cushions and some rope from the basement. There.

I squeeze through the front door and begin my chase. I don't seem to be going very fast, though. The cushions are slowing down my superspeed.

Gurk! The animal control van is already long gone, and I don't know where the headquarters are!

Think, Marty. Jerome's depending on you.

I know. I can use my powerful canine nose to track Jerome!

I stand by the curb and smell the air.

Nothing. Except maybe pizza with ham, pineapple, and extra cheese, but that's not very helpful.

Maybe I need to smell the ground. That's what dogs do.

I lean over sideways to put my nose closer to the pavement but lose my balance.

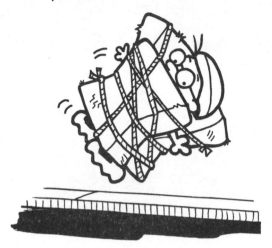

I end up flat on my back.

I try to roll over, but I can't move!

I'm like an upside-down turtle!

And I can't get loose because I tied the knots too tight with my superhuman strength!

I stare up at the darkening sky and wonder what happens now.

It's *my* fault that Jerome was taken. What are they going to do with him?

They don't understand him like I do!

And here I am, seconds away from transforming into a vicious menace to society. Will I even remember what happens tonight?

I've never felt this helpless . . . this hopeless.

Wait, I'm catching a whiff of something. Is it Jerome?
No.
Smells more like B.O.

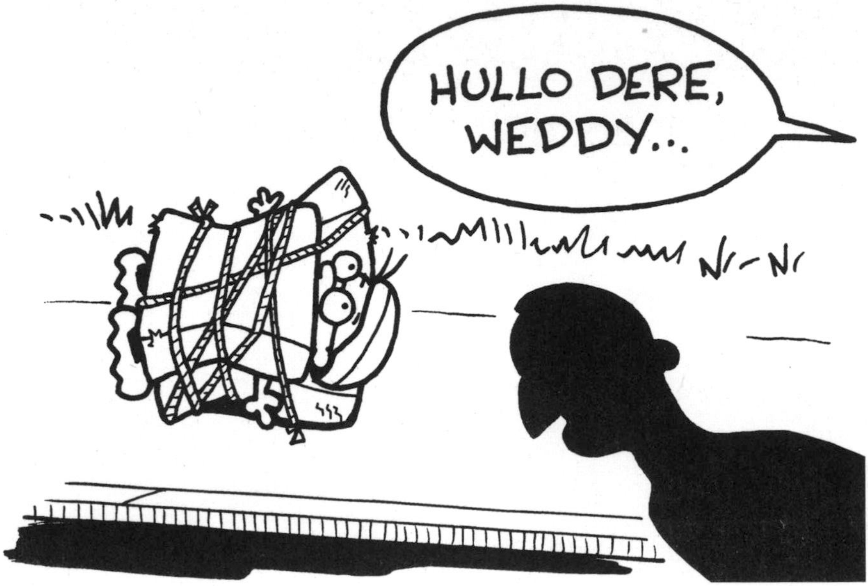
HULLO DERE,
WEDDY...

CHAPTER 35
it goes downhill from here

Peach Fuzz! Not my first choice, but maybe I can get him to help me!

"Dressin up earlee for Hullaween, Weddy Pants?" He doesn't realize I'm about to turn into a werewolf. I better warn him.

"If you don't help me out of this," I say, "I might just rip off your head."

"Har ho heh har!" Peach Fuzz laughs. "Soundz like ya needz ta be tawt anotha lessun!"

Peach Fuzz pushes me with his foot and rolls me across the grass.

"I tried to warn you, Peach Fuzz."

"Wut did ya calls me?!"

I've never called him Peach Fuzz to his face before, but with all my werewolf powers, I'm not scared of him anymore.

"I called you Peach Fuzz because of your stupid peach-fuzz mustache!"

"Oh, Weddy, Weddy, Weddy. Yer gonna get it now." Peach Fuzz stands over me and scrunches up his mouth.

Eww! He's about to drop a spit wad on my face! I can't move my arms, but I can move my jaw.

That tastes worse than my mom's fish casserole!

"OWAAAUARGH! Ya liddle . . ." Peach Fuzz screams as he hops around holding his leg.

He falls backward into me, and I bounce a few feet away. I start to spin slowly, then really, really FAST!

What's going on? Is this what it's like to transform into a werewolf?

Gurk! I'm completely out of control!

It feels like being trapped on a broken carnival ride! Things whiz by so fast, all I can see are blurred images.

I catch glimpses of rocks, trees, and small animals. Then I notice sidewalks, cars, and buildings. Suddenly, I burst through some big double doors and slowly come to a stop in the middle of a crowded room.

It takes a second for my dizzy eyes to focus.

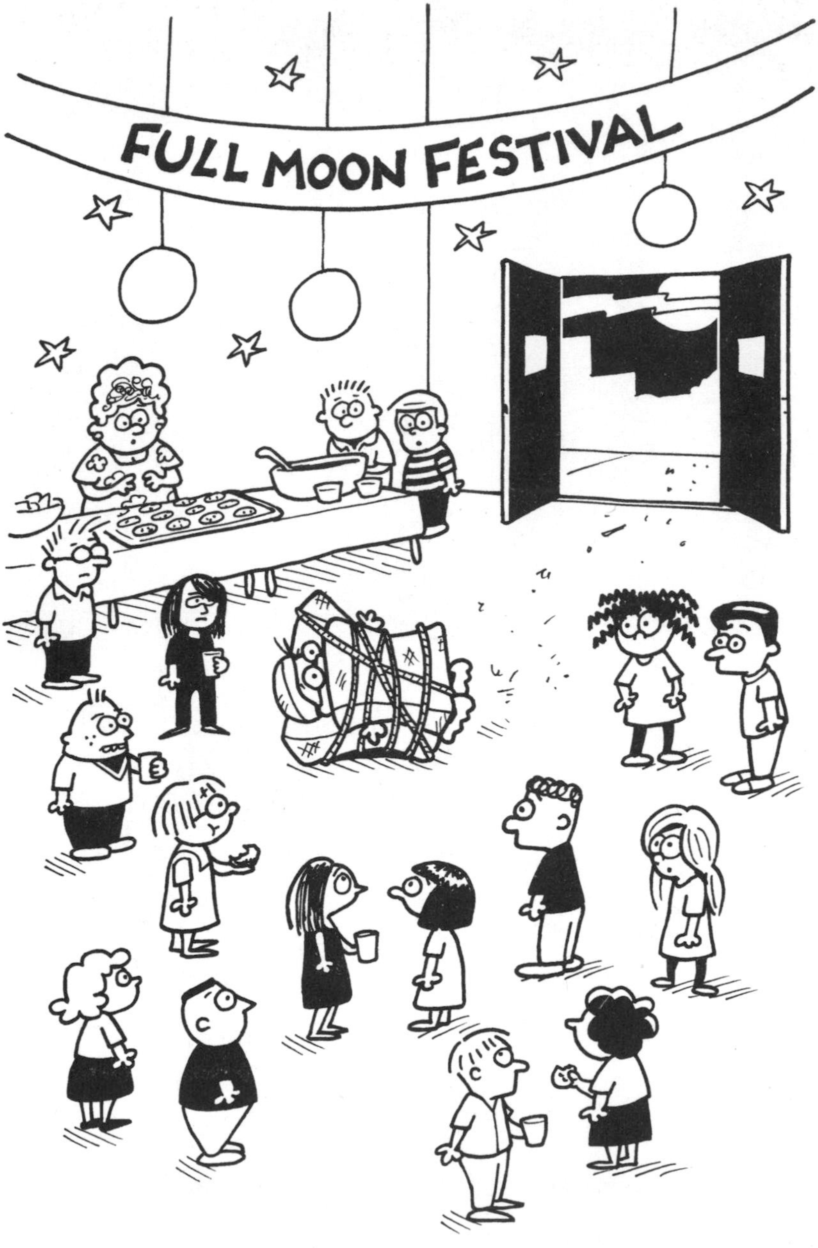
FULL MOON FESTIVAL

CHAPTER 36
bite me

Oh no!

I'm about to turn into a werewolf in front of the WHOLE SCHOOL!

What if I get loose and bite everybody? I hope they took baths! And there's Parker! What if I attack her?

BWA HA HA!

"Nice of you to wear your formal couch cushions, Marty!" Simon says between laughs. "I always knew you were soft!"

Parker gives Simon a dirty look and comes over to help me to my feet. The ropes have loosened.

"GET BACK, EVERYONE!" I yell. "FOR YOUR OWN SAFETY!"

They all just stare at me.

"Ooooh, Marty!" Simon says. "I'm so scared of the creepy couch creature!"

I hear three giggles, two chuckles, and a guffaw.

"THIS IS NOT A DRILL!" I announce. "GET BACK OR GET BITTEN!"

The laughter gets louder.

No one seems to be taking the situation seriously! Parker stays next to me, trying to undo the ropes. That's the exact *wrong* thing to do!

"PARKER!" I shout. "STOP IT! GET AWAY FROM ME!"

She keeps working on the ropes.

"Please, Parker," I say desperately. "You're the last person I want to hurt."

I manage to get a hand free and push her away, for her own safety.

I look over at the doors I just smashed through. Outside I can see the night sky.

And there it is!

THE FULL MOON.

The energy in the room quickly changes. I feel myself shaking uncontrollably!

"Marty!" Parker says. "What's happening to you?"

I shake more and more. I can't help it!

All the laughing in the room suddenly stops. And then . . .

Everyone stares in disbelief! Ms. Ortiz screams!

"WATCH OUT, EVERYONE!" she shouts. "DON'T LET HIM BITE YOU! GET TO SAFETY!"

Kids and adults run away in every direction, climbing on chairs and tables.

It's chaos!

And Parker is still on the floor next to me!

I open my mouth to tell Parker to run away as fast as she can, but all I hear is . . .

But that howl didn't come from me.

There's something else stuck here in the cushions with me! It's been making me shake as it struggles to get out!

It leaps to the floor and circles around the room.

It's Dewey! But something's different.

He doesn't look sweet anymore—he looks dangerous!

And he's heading straight for Parker, who still hasn't moved! She seems confused. Dewey leaps at Parker with his jaws wide open!

I step sideways to shield Parker from Dewey.

The little dog sinks his fangs into the couch cushions. He doesn't let go.

"Is that . . . Dewey?" Parker asks as she peeks from behind me. "What's gotten into him?!"

The animal control guy comes rushing in. "Now I got you, you little bugger!"

He grabs Dewey with a loop on a long pole and pulls him off me.

"Hey, kid!" he says. "Thanks for helping me catch this pesky critter!"

"But I wasn't trying to . . ."

"And thanks for the tip about that crazy feral cat! He really put up a fight!"

"That cat's not feral!" I snap. "He's JEROME! My PET! You weren't supposed to take HIM! You were supposed to take ME!"

"You?"

"Yes! I'm a WEREWOLF!"

"You look like a normal kid to me," he says.

"I do?"

"Well, not the way you're dressed," he adds.

The animal control guy struggles with Dewey and drags him outside.

I waddle over to the punch bowl and peek at my reflection.

He's right. I didn't transform.

Why not? This makes no sense!

But I can't worry about that right now. I have someone to rescue!

I dash outside to the animal control van, leaving a trail of rope and cushions behind me.

And there's my best friend trapped behind bars. I open the cage.

CHAPTER 37

the marty remains the same

I hold Jerome and stare up at the starry, starry night.

There's the moon.

There are no clouds in front of it or anything. It's as full as a full moon can be.

And here I am, completely human.

Is it possible that all of this was my imagination and I was never a werewolf to begin with?

Nah. There has to be a logical explanation.

"Thank you, Marty," Parker says as she joins me.

"Just glad you're okay," I tell her.

"What's Jerome doing here?"

"Long story," I say.

Parker looks over at the animal control guy. "What happens to Dewey now?" she asks me.

"Good question. I'll find out."

I walk back to the van as Dewey is being locked in one of the cages. That little dog is not happy.

"What's next for Dewey?" I ask him.

"Dewey?" says the animal control guy.

"That little dog. My friend named him Dewey."

"Well, he looks pretty dangerous, so . . ."

"Could you take him to my vet?" I ask.

"Your vet?"

"Well, my cat's vet. Dr. Orr. If she can handle Jerome, she can handle anything!"

"That's not usually how it works, kid. If an animal is considered to be a danger . . ."

"You broke into my house and kidnapped my cat!" I remind him. "Plus, I'm the one who helped you catch Dewey in the first place. You owe me."

"Fine, kid," he says. "Dewey can be your vet's problem."

We shake on it.

The van drives off, and Parker watches until it disappears out of sight.

We go back inside, and I get some pats on the back. Needless to say, the event ends early, but not before Parker and I are named king and queen of the Full Moon Festival.

CHAPTER 38

the cure

I take a seat while Parker calls her dad.

Ms. Ortiz comes over to me. "How are you doing, Marty? That was very brave of you back there."

She hands me a candy bar.

Ms. Ortiz always knows the right thing to do.

Wait.

Candy.

I'm having the epiphany of all epiphanies!

The reason I'm not a werewolf is *CANDY*! Candy gave me a cavity.

So I went to the dentist and got a filling. A *silver* filling.

They say that the best way to defeat a werewolf is with a silver bullet, right? Well, a silver filling obviously works the same way. Except, instead of getting vanquished, I got cured.

Candy. Is there anything it can't do?

CHAPTER 39

slow ride

I get a ride from Parker and her dad. Roongrat comes with us, too.

But not Simon.

In the car, Parker makes a lot of dramatic gestures while she gives her dad the play-by-play of the evening. But it's hard to hear everything from the back seat, especially with Roongrat talking.

"So, Marty," Mr. Fedora says, "I'm told that you make a nice-looking couch!"

"Um . . ."

"Seriously, though, thanks for watching out for my daughter."

"She watches out for me all the time," I tell him.

"I'll swing by your house so you can clean up and drop off your cat before I bring you to Roongrat's."

"Thanks, Mr. Fedora. We've both had a long night."

We stop at a traffic light, and I notice two figures walking.

One of them is Peach Fuzz. And he's whining. "But MUUUUUM!"

"You were bitten on the ankle by something, dear," Mother Ack tells her son. "You could get rabies or whatnot. I'm taking you to the emergency room to get a series of very painful shots, Salvador."

"Butt I alreadee got dose shotz!"

"I insist you have them again, dear. Just to be safe. You know how I worry."

"It wuz Weddy Pantz who bit mee! WEDDY PANTZ TYED UP IN COWCH COOSHUNS!!"

"Hush, dear. You're delirious . . ."

CHAPTER 40

we can be heroes

"You slept late!" Roongrat's mother tells me in the morning.*

She makes us waffles.

"Thank you, Ms. Mitten."

"Marty," she says, "did you know the first waffles were made of tree bark? They were called 'awfuls.' That's a fact."

It's a relief not being a werewolf anymore. Sure, I miss the superhuman powers, but there was a lot of stress and responsibility involved.

* Technically, afternoon.

Who needs that?

Before I head home, Roongrat and I play another game of *Dragon Eater.*

It's a close one, but I win.*

"Thanks for not eating me," Roongrat says.

"You're welcome, Roonie."

Ms. Mitten drops me off at home, and my dad greets me at the door.

"What happened while we were gone, Marty?"

"Jerome had a rough night," I say.

"Is there anything else you want to tell me?"

"Why do you ask?"

"Half the couch is missing."

"Oh, that. It's a long story, but I come out a hero," I explain. "Just ask Ms. Ortiz."

* Of course.

"I'm not sure I want to know," my dad says. "Come on, Marty. We've got a lot of work to do before your mother gets back."

When my mom comes home that evening, I'm not the only hero. My dad's one, too.

He bought a new couch.

My mom's also a hero. She landed a new client, and based on her reaction, I think it means a raise.

As for Erica, she's a hero in her own mind.

A trophy and a medal? Seems excessive.

Now that I think about it, coming in first place in a History Trivia Contest is quite an accomplishment for my sister, considering she was worrying about me becoming a werewolf the whole time.

What impressive concentration skills.

In fact, she must *still* be worried about me being a monster. She doesn't know the danger is over.

It's time for me to clue her in.

"Hey, Erica! Look at my silver filling. My *silver* filling. Made of *silver*."

"You're such a weirdo," she says.

She got the message. She understands that I'm fully cured of my werewolfism.

How do I know? I can see an epiphany in the way she rolls her eyes.

CHAPTER 41

the sweetest thing

As promised, the animal control guy lets my vet check out Dewey.

She discovers he isn't rabid.

"It's the weirdest thing," Dr. Orr says. "We found something inside Dewey's brain that we've never seen before. We removed it and discovered it only affected him during a full moon. Made him aggressive with wolflike tendencies."

"So he's healthy now?" Parker asks.

"Very healthy. We'll watch him for a while, but I imagine he'll be ready for adoption soon."

"Really?"

"Now that he doesn't have that mysterious mutant thing in his head, he's a sweetheart."

He certainly looks different all cleaned up.

"What was the thing you found?" Parker's dad asks.

"No idea," Dr. Orr says. "Strange, though. Some men in sunglasses and dark suits came by and took it with them."

I'm only half listening.

Parker has been jumping up and down ever since the vet said "adoption."

"I'd adopt him myself if I didn't already have eight dogs," Dr. Orr says. "And nineteen cats."

"Dad, can we adopt him. Pleeeeeeeeeease!" Parker begs.

"Tell you what, Parker, let's just wait till the next full moon. If he's still this sweet, he's yours."

"Really?!"

"Really."

"Thankyouthankyouthankyou!"

"One more thing," Parker's dad says as he turns to Dr. Orr. "That surgery couldn't have been cheap. Who paid for it?"

"Marty did."

Parker and her dad look at me.

"I know what it's like to love an animal," I say. "And Parker really loves Dewey, so it was money well spent." Parker kisses me on the cheek.*

It was money very, very, very, very, very well spent.

---

* This kiss was way better than the time Dewey kissed me. And not just because Parker's breath is significantly better than Dewey's. Although that is a factor. After all, Dewey's breath was pretty rank. I mean, nastier than Jerome's breath after he's eaten a can of Fisherman's Catch cat food. So, although the breath remains a factor, it's not the biggest factor in which kiss I enjoyed more. But I digress. Let's get back to the part about me paying for Dewey's surgery.

CHAPTER 42
sign me up

"How did you afford it?" Parker's dad asks me on the way home. "That surgery must have been expensive."

I explain that I recently received a hefty sum of cash.

Remember that graffiti I drew on The Candy Factory building?

Well, look where else I noticed it.

Turns out the important-looking man who gave me the compliments was The Candy Factory president. He liked my Mr. Candy drawing so much, he immediately used it on billboards to promote his company.

Without paying me.

So I stopped by with my lawyer.

"The legal ramifications contrastingly applied to procedural legitimacy of copyright enunciation heretofore encapsulated in all furthermore publication provisions . . ."

Anyway, we negotiated a firm but fair deal and I was well compensated for my art. Just like an artist should be.

Of course, we agreed that some of my payment would come in a form other than money.

Plus they covered my lawyer's fees.

CHAPTER 43
oh snap

Parker, Roongrat, and I meet at the common. I brought my school photos, and they're trying to help me decide which one's the best.

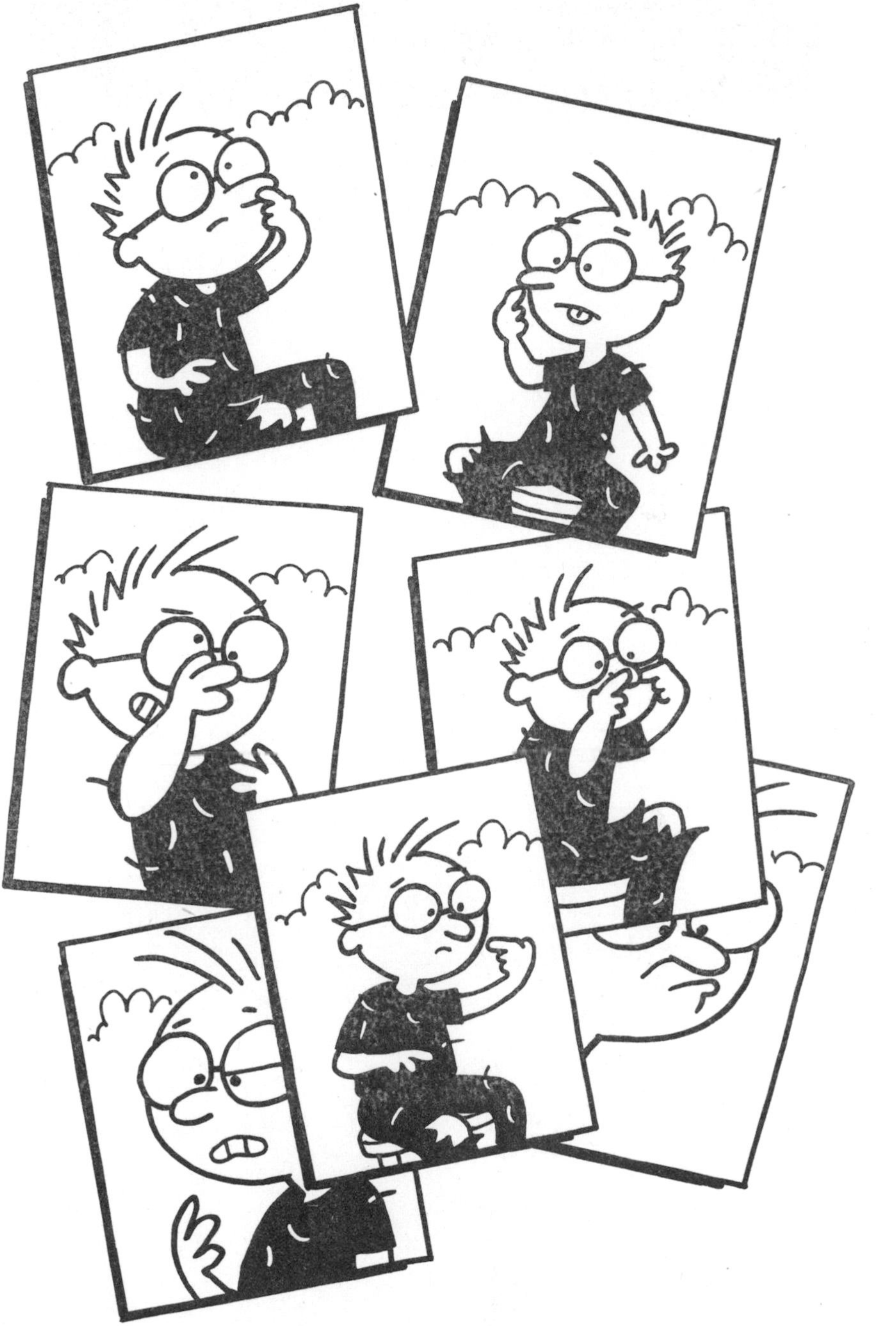

"They all have personality!" Parker says.

I make it a point not to argue with people when they're right.

Although my mom had a different reaction when she saw the pics.

"HEY, SIMON!" Roongrat shouts.

Simon's walking on the other side of the street, and Roonie's trying to get his attention.

Simon gives a reluctant wave and keeps on walking.

"Did you see Simon's photos?" Roongrat asks us. "They're truculent!"

None of us knows what that means, especially Roongrat.

Simon's been in a bad mood since the Full Moon Festival. Not sure why.

It could be because I saved the day.

It could be because Parker's not paying much attention to him anymore.

It could be because The Candy Factory paid me for my art, which means I am now literally, actually, and officially something he said I could never be.

A PROFESSIONAL ARTIST!

Or it could be something else.

Since the Candy Factory never asked for my permission before publishing my art on their billboards, I was able to talk them into giving me an extra bonus. I got to use one of their billboards any way I wanted!

And I decided to express myself.

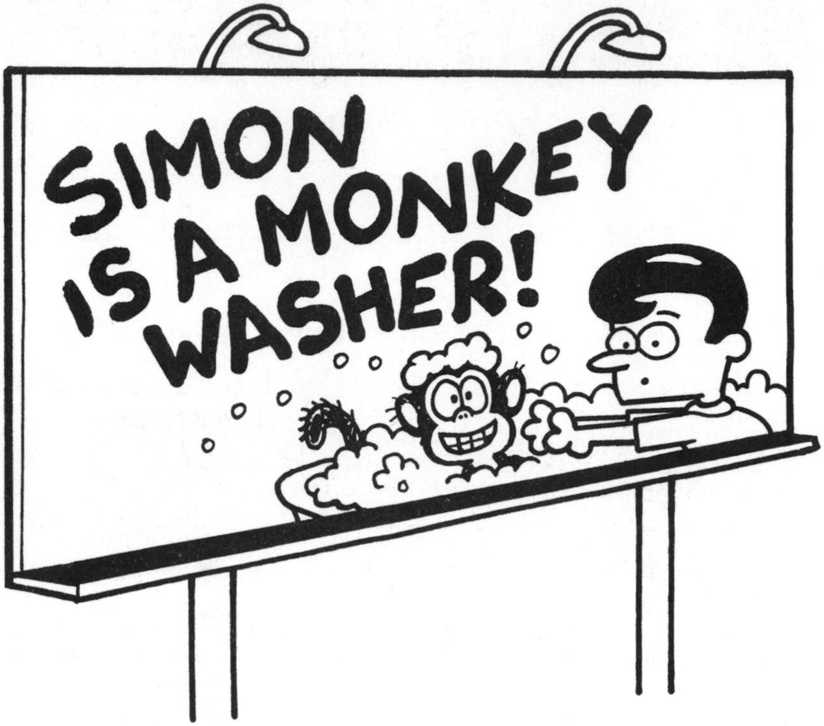
SIMON
IS A MONKEY
WASHER!

CHAPTER 14

head home

Everything's pretty much back to normal, except for one thing.

Jerome's still hiding under my bed instead of sleeping on my head. Can't he sense I'm no longer a werewolf?

I reach under my bed with some fresh catnip and try to reassure him that I'm 100 percent human. I notice he's busy chewing on something.

Wow!

Jerome had it the whole time!

He must have rescued it from the candy box and dragged it under my bed.

Erica is going to be so relieved!

But she's not going to be happy about the condition. Jerome gnawed right through the strap.

And the strap was the only thing that kept someone else from reading it.

Which means there's nothing to stop me now. I'll finally be able to see all the secrets my sister wrote about me!

I retrieve something from my nightstand. The piece of paper that started this whole thing.

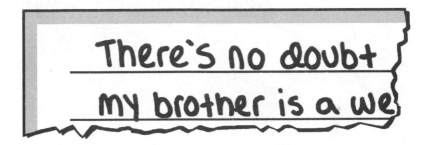

There's no doubt
my brother is a we

Then I flip through the diary and find a page with the top torn off.

I line up the ripped edges and . . . voilà!

They fit together!

Wait.

> ## There's no doubt my brother is a weirdo, but I love him anyway.

It says nothing about me being a werewolf. How can that be?

Something's not right.

Then I have one final epiphany. This isn't the right page!

The rest of the *real* page doesn't exist anymore because it ended up somewhere else.

So that explains that.

Well, since it's here, I might as well read the rest of the diary.

I'm sure there is all kinds of intriguing information in there that Erica doesn't want me to know.

I settle into bed, turn to page one, and start reading.

"Dear Diary, today I . . ."

The book is suddenly yanked out of my hands.

Jerome scampers out of the room with it in his mouth. Then I hear a voice in the hall.

"Is that . . . ? IT IS! MY DIARY! GIVE ME THAT, YOU LITTLE . . . !"

There's some kind of scuffle, and then it gets quiet. Too quiet.

Then Jerome struts back into my room, hops on the bed, and nestles on top of my head.

He seems ready for a good night's sleep.

Okay, now things are officially back to normal. Everything is back where it's supposed to be. There's finally peace in the universe.

Well, not peace exactly.

Because the house feels like it's shaking.

The sound of stomping sister feet seems to be getting closer and closer.

Louder and louder.

Angrier and angrier.

I think the smartest course of action would be to pretend I'm asleep, so I have to stop writing now.

Good night. Marty Pants out.
For now.

THE END

Find out what Marty is up to
in his next adventure:

HOW TO DEFEAT A WIZARD

CHAPTER 1
sorry not sorry

Apologize to Simon?

I can think of a few things I'd rather do than apologize to Simon.

1. Run naked through a cactus patch. (Without sunscreen.)

2. Eat a raw porcupine.
(Without ketchup.)*

* Or catsup.

3. Listen to my dad talk about old music. (Without a pillow.)

But Principal Cricklewood isn't impressed with any of these options. She insists I apologize to Simon.

For what?

All I did was call Simon a

MONKEY WASHER!

And I'm not even sure what it means. I just like the way it sounds.

I tried to explain to Principal Cricklewood that being called a monkey washer could be a compliment.

But something she said gave me the impression she wasn't buying it.

It's not fair. Simon insults me all the time but gets away with it because he's sneaky. He tricks people.

Even my mom falls for it.

A lot of people call Simon charming. Charming, charming, charming.

I'm sick of hearing it.

Just for kicks, I hop on my dad's computer and look up "charming" to see if there's any possible definition that could apply to Simon.

charm-ing:
1. delightful, pleasant, likeable, adorable

Ugh! Stop!

Simon is so *not* charming. How has he tricked people into thinking he's charming?

Hold on. There's another definition.

charm-ing:

2. the act of using magic powers

Whoa.

Could Simon have *magic powers*?

READ THEM ALL!

Follow Marty Pants as
he saves the world again . . .

. . . and again . . . and again . . .

Praise for the Marty Pants series

About the Author

After many odd jobs and a graphic design degree, Mark Parisi created the *Off the Mark* comic strip series in 1987. It is syndicated in more than one hundred newspapers around the country and has twice won the Best Newspaper Panel Award from the National Cartoonists Society. Marty Pants is his debut book series. Mark lives in Massachusetts and is most likely covered in cat fur.